Watching
and other Stories

Margaret Holbrook

ISBN-10: 1484982444
ISBN-13: 978-1484982440

This book is dedicated to
Mum and Dad
Ste and Ben

With Love.

ABOUT THIS BOOK…

This is a collection of short stories and flash fiction. It includes some pieces that will make the reader think, and some that are a lighter read.

The title story in the collection, *Watching*, is about that human trait of observing others.

The longest piece in the book, *Reflections of Murder*, is a novella.

The short story, *The Little Black Dress*, was written with several Buckinghamshire villages in mind. My father hailed from Maids Moreton.

Jane Said, the final story in the book, is a piece of flash fiction. It is always well received. Most people seem to find an affinity with the 8 year old 'little sister'.

CONTENTS

1 WATCHING

I've been watching and wondering about you now for a couple of months. You're always in the cafe when I arrive for my morning drink. My morning drink in this particular cafe is taken on a Tuesday. You sit in the lower area by the till. I always sit in the raised balcony area. I always arrive at 11.35 am. I note that you are dressed as usual in your green combat jacket. Odd I suspect for someone of your age, (late forties early fifties). As usual your collar is up, as if turned against the cold but we're inside, it isn't cold, not in here. In fact for the time of year it's unseasonably warm. You have just picked up the paperback book that is always placed on the table to the left of your tray. You have eaten sandwiches for your lunch today. The wrappers are on the tray next to the empty cup. You never move the tray. You leave everything on it as you lunch, everything that is apart from the book. The book I have seen you take from the inside pocket of your jacket. It seems to be one of the first things you do as you sit down. It forms for you, I think, some kind of ritual. The book sits on the table and waits patiently while you eat. I have observed that if the weather is cold or wet it is a soup lunch. If it is warm, as it is today, sandwiches are your choice. The drink never changes, that I can see is always coffee.

You are reading your book now and are totally engrossed. I cannot glimpse the title, but such is the book's grip on you that you seem oblivious to the noise and the people moving around you. I take another drink of my coffee, it is particularly good today. There was a new girl serving, 'Barista, Hannah', it said on her badge. I thought that as she was new, the coffee might not be up to standard, I am proved wrong, and pleasantly so. I replace my cup on the saucer and glance downward. I try to see if I can figure out the colour of your eyes. I can't. You have slitty eyes, narrow eyes. Your hair is grey and thinning. I fancy that you should have pale blue or grey eyes. They shouldn't be dark at all. It wouldn't suit. I lean back in my seat and continue to watch. I see you each week but have never seen you with anyone. It doesn't seem to matter how long I stay, you are always alone at your table.
I've been here over forty minutes now. You are still reading.

You have become an obsession with me. I am sure there is more to you. There must be. No one has such an ordinary existence, no one. What is your secret, Mr. Green? Mr. Green, I call you that because of the colour of your jacket. I do not know your name. What is your secret? I'm sure there must be one, must be something more to you than this. I determine to find out. It may mean that I have to forgo my balcony seat, that I sit a little closer to you. Shall I? Yes, next week. Next Tuesday I shall start to discover your secret Mr. Green, start to discover what makes you tick.

Tuesday arrives and I take my seat in the lower cafe area. I sit a few tables away from you. I take a magazine from my bag and begin to read. Occasionally I glance across. Nothing changes. You've had your lunch and drink, the wrappers and cup are on the tray, you are reading your book. The weeks pass by as I watch you, Mr. Green. The routine is the same. The only thing to change is the book. No one speaks to you and no one joins you. You are a solitary man, Mr. Green.

It is June now and very hot. I take off the silver grey jacket that I am wearing and place it over the back of the chair. The coffee is excellent, as it has been ever since the advent of Hannah. I am drawing a blank as far as you are concerned. I think you will end up my spring/summer obsession. I will not go into autumn like this!

A lady comes across to '*my table*', 'do you mind if I join you, there isn't a space anywhere. It's so busy today.'

She has already put her tray down on the table. I nod my head in assent. I hope she doesn't want to talk. Mr. Green is reading his book. She looks at me as I glance over in his direction and smiles.

'He reads a lot, Frank, and writes too. I think he comes here for inspiration.' I look blankly at her,

'Sorry? I say, 'do you know him?'

'Neighbours, he and his wife live in the same village.'

I look questioningly, 'Village?'

'Yes, well I suppose it isn't a village, not any more, Marple Bridge, but we like to think it is.'

'He's here every Tuesday when I call in for coffee.'

'As I said, I think he comes here for inspiration.'

'I don't think it would inspire me. It can get very noisy, particularly in school holidays.'

'Writers are a different bunch. They can shut off all noise. Escape into them-selves if they need to.'

I nod. I can't really stay much longer. I gather my things together and prepare to leave.

'Well, it's been nice talking to you, what did you say his name was?'

'Frank, Frank Hyde.'

The next week when I took my seat in the cafe Mr. Green wasn't there. Two more Tuesdays came and went and still no Mr. Green. I decided I should go to Marple Bridge. It was quiet when I arrived. I parked my car and sat for a minute or two, honestly, what was I doing here? I didn't know where to go. I could hardly go round knocking on doors and asking for him. It was lunchtime and I was hungry. I went to a pub by the river. I sat down at a table by the window. The menu was basic but acceptable. I ordered my meal and then sat idly gazing round. While I was waiting I heard a man shout 'Frank.' I turned round hurriedly almost knocking the wine glass from the table, such was my panic. It wasn't 'my Frank' though. It was a total stranger. By now, even though I had never spoken to 'Mr. Green', I did not consider us strangers.

When I had finished eating and the waitress came to clear the table, I mentioned to her Frank Hyde's name, did she know him?

'Frank the writer?'

'Yes.' All the time thinking, '*everyone seems to know Frank.*'

'He lives in a cottage up Holker Lane.'

'Really, is that far?'

'No. Turn right out of here and up the hill. You'll see his cottage on the right. It's the last one before the farm.'

I didn't know what to do. My game was virtually over, at its close. I knew Mr. Green's name, I knew what he did for a living. What more was there to know? If I met him would I speak? It was all like being in a fantasy. I was creating another world in my head.

I walked up the main street and the thoughts were still playing around. I decided I would go and see where he lived. It would complete my picture of him. I owed myself that much.

The cottage was ordinary, very ordinary. In fact it looked as though it could do with a coat of paint. Perhaps book sales were slow? The garden was kempt, after a fashion. It was quiet, no one around. I stood for a few minutes just looking at the cottage. I was disturbed in my silent thoughts by the sound of someone shouting, 'You, what you doin'? Need any help?

I was confronted by a ruddy faced middle aged woman, perhaps not the full money. She sported a brown woollen hat which added to the oddness of her appearance, particularly as it was by now late summer. 'I'm fine, thank you, just out for a walk.' At once her gaze went downwards. I was wearing blue wedge sandals, and I was smartly dressed. Not walking attire at all. I smiled and turned, hearing her call after me,

'Frank's not in. We get a lot of your sort up here, noseying.'

I walked down into Marple Bridge, got into my car and drove home. Fantasy over.

The next Tuesday I didn't call for coffee, but at the beginning of August I went into the cafe and sat in the balcony area. I was lucky to get a seat. It was school holidays and the place was full of mums and children. I glanced downward to the lower seating area. Mr. Green wasn't there. I felt empty and a surge of sadness overcame me. It was as if part of my life was gone. It was as if Mr. Green had never existed, as if I had made him up, a figment of my imagination. I didn't visit the café for the next few weeks, it would be September before I returned.

When I did return it was much quieter, the holidays having finished, and as soon as I sat down, Hannah approached me. She had a package in her hand.

'Mr Hyde asked if we could give you this. Sorry it's a bit late but we haven't seen you for a while. We weren't sure at first whether it was for you or not, but he said 'yes', you were to have it.'

Hannah must have noted my puzzled look.

'Funny as well, he knew your name.' Hannah pointed to the label, 'Miss Grey', it read.

'That's not my name,' I answered, 'but I think I know what he means.'

It was Hannah's turn to look puzzled now as she left me to open the package. It was a book, there was a note attached,

Dear Miss Grey, I hope you will accept this gift. You may not realise it, but over spring you were my inspiration.'

Regards, Frank Hyde.

I looked at the book. It was entitled 'Watching'. I opened it and turned to the first chapter, it began;

You are there again Miss Grey, sipping coffee and trying not to be noticed as you sit in your balcony seat. I don't know your name. I call you Miss Grey because of the jacket you wear, fair weather or foul. It is always coffee that you drink, I know that. I have been watching you over the last few weeks and it is always the same. You are always alone. You never meet anyone or come in with anyone. You are a solitary woman. What makes you tick Miss Grey? I determine to find out. No one can have such an ordinary existence, no one. What is your secret Miss Grey?

2 RETIREMENT BLUES

Edna had assumed that when Jim retired he would take up golf. He'd played occasionally and had even talked of taking up membership of the local golf club when there was a vacancy. His name was on the waiting list, he had proposers and seconders lined up. There never seemed to be a vacancy. Jim wasn't downhearted although Edna sensed some frustration there. Jim was a man of few words. Edna had learnt this through thirty- five years of marriage. It was no use pushing him. He would sort things out in his own time. It was what he did. Unbeknown to Edna, Jim had a secret he had never in all their thirty-five years of marriage revealed to her. The first Edna knew of this was when Jim returned home after his last working day at 'Oldham and Longshanks', chartered surveyors.

'Hello love', he said as he walked through the door. Edna thought he sounded sheepish.

'Maybe had a little too much to drink', she

thought.

His head appeared first, round the door, his hands and lower body being obscured by the door, as if hiding something.

'Come in' Edna said, 'you're a retired person now, you can do whatever you like.'

Jim stalled. He had never told his wife this particular secret. How would she react?

'Are you all right Jim?' Edna asked, 'you seem...odd.'

'Yes,' came the reply.

'Well come in then, we can't stay like this all evening, the dinner will spoil. It's your favourite, chicken casserole.'

'Lovely. Thanks love.'

'Jim, for goodness sake come and sit down, tell me about this afternoon, the drinks with your colleagues, how did it go, what did they get you?'

Jim gulped. Edna had always been like this, one sentence could become a list of instructions or a series of questions. He'd always felt, right from the very early days of their marriage that if he didn't answer correctly, or answered out of order, he was doomed. Jim gulped again and entered the room. He was carrying quite a large case. It was blue with a silver/grey trim. From the way Jim carried it, Edna could see there was some weight to it. Edna peered over the top of her glasses. Jim didn't like it when she did this. He felt as though he were back at school and about to be charged with some minor misdemeanour. Edna could see there was a name on one side of the case. It didn't mean anything to her. There was a pause in the conversation, less than a minute but Jim felt trapped. As if he had fallen into a chasm and couldn't get out. Edna broke the silence

'Jim, what's the matter? Is that your gift? Let me see, it looks impressive.'

'*Oh no*,' thought Jim, '*she's off again. Firing me a line of questions. What do I say?*'

Jim gulped again and sat down. Not on the sofa next to Edna but on one of the chairs. He thought he'd be better on his own, more under control. He placed the case on the floor between his legs. He felt that would protect it somehow from the response he was expecting from Edna.

'Aren't you going to show me?' Edna said.

'Show you what?' Jim replied.

'Your gift, what is it?'

'Oh yes, the gift,' mumbled Jim, 'yes, this is my gift from my work colleagues. I'll say now that it's something I've always wanted, and I'm going to make use of it throughout my retirement. It may surprise you Edna but...' Jim paused as he opened the case to reveal the saxophone.

Edna gasped, 'a saxophone! I didn't know you played.'

'I don't,' replied Jim, 'but I'm going to learn.'

When Edna had thought about Jim's retirement she imagined golf club dinners, ladies' coffee mornings. It wasn't to be. Jim joined a saxophone band. They met every Saturday morning at a local school. They played for an hour with a break for coffee and talk of other '*muso's*'. For once in his life Jim had 'friends' that were his. He didn't share these friends with Edna. It felt great!

After a few weeks, Jim decided to have lessons. This meant he was now out of the house on Wednesday mornings. Edna didn't mind. She'd always thought men, '*rather got under one's feet'*.

Frankie, Jim's teacher was a young woman in her thirties. She said Jim had '*natural talent'*. It boosted his confidence immensely. Jim arrived home after his lessons a new man. Edna, although she would never admit it, was a little put out by her husband's new found '*joie de vivre'*.

Jim's Saturday group was taken by a young man named Kevin, Kevo to the boys. Kevo had high hopes for the band. There were ten sax players, all of varying abilities. There were a couple of tenors, a bass, five altos, a baritone and a soprano. The mix wasn't perfect but they didn't sound bad.

'In another couple of months maybe we'll 'do a gig', Kevo announced one morning.

'Do you think we're up to it?' Jim asked, 'only I'm fairly new to this game.'

'You'll be fine, all of you, don't worry,' Kevo replied, 'I have great faith in my '*Swing 'n' Sax'*.'

Jim still had to tell Edna the band had a name. It was just another one of those things that he'd '*have to get round to'*. On Saturday when Jim returned from band Edna '*had it on her'*.

'Enjoyed yourself have you? Did you play all right? What did 'Kevo' have to say?

'*Good heavens*,' Jim thought, '*she can't stop herself can she?*'

It was true, she couldn't, but she had had years of practice.

'I've been here on my own, a saxophone

widow,' she said, and then carried on again, 'if you'd taken up golf as I expected, at least I'd have got something out of it. The golf club dinner for instance, from this I get nothing.'

'Ah, well,' Jim replied, 'that's where you're wrong. We're putting a set together for a gig. Don't know where yet. Kevo's arranging it.'

'What!' Edna replied in amazement, 'Ten old men playing saxophones, who'll pay for that?'

Jim decided now was the time, 'We're the 'Swing 'n' Sax',' Jim said with pride, 'and Kevo thinks we'll be fine.''

'But you're still having lessons, you'll make a mess of it, you'll be an embarrassment."

'I won't. We carry each other and once we've got the set rehearsed, Kevo says we'll be fine.'

Over the next six weeks Edna got used to hearing Jim rehearse. She became familiar with the names of jazz classics, Satin Doll, Basin Street Blues and Take the 'A' Train. Edna found she quite liked listening to Jim's playing.

One Saturday when Jim returned from practice Edna was in a fairly happy mood.

'Do you and the boys ever play 'Moonlight in Vermont'?' she asked.

'We haven't, but I'm sure I could get the music for it.'

'It's a favourite of mine,' Edna replied, 'I'm surprised you don't remember.'

It was true. How could he have forgotten? Jim looked at Edna and smiled. The next week he asked Frankie if she had a copy of '*Moonlight in Vermont'*, he could borrow. She hadn't, but sent him off to the music shop in town saying, *'tell them Frankie sent you and you'll get a discount.'*

Having got the music, Jim practised every moment he could. He'd wait until Edna had gone out and then he was away. Practice, practice, practice!

A few weeks later Edna asked, 'When's the gig then?'

'Would you be interested in coming?' Jim asked.

'Of course, after all, my husband's a *muso* and a member of '*Swing 'n' Sax'*.'

Jim smiled. Edna could be wonderful. He'd forgotten that as well.

'Two weeks tonight,' he said, 'we're playing upstairs at the '*Black Swan'*. It'll be a good night. I'm glad you want to come.'

The next week when Jim went for his lesson he played '*Moonlight in Vermont'*, and Frankie said '*not bad'*.

When Jim arrived home he was so full of himself he felt he might burst. He was smiling broadly as he walked into the lounge.

'Edna, I've got a surprise for you. Stay where you are. I'll just get set up.'

When Jim started to play, Edna couldn't believe it,

'Jim it's wonderful.'

And it was. Jim was note perfect.

'I've been practising every moment I had, I wanted it to be a surprise.'

'Oh, Jim.'

That was the reaction he'd wanted.

'Play it through again, Jim.'

He did, and Edna began to sing,

'icy finger waves, ski trails down a mountain side, snow time in Vermont.'

'Edna, I've not heard you sing in a long time. You used to sing all the time when we were first married.'

'I know Jim, a lot of water under the bridge since then. Anyway, that was lovely. I'm so looking forward to Saturday night.'

When Saturday arrived the band practised as usual. Kevo told them he was sure '*the evening would be a resounding success, were they up for it?'*

They were!

Jim and Edna left home in plenty of time. Edna wanted to be sure of a good seat. Edna chose her table and Jim bought them both a drink. She was nervous, nervous for both of them. She knew that tonight meant so much to Jim. By eight-thirty the room was getting full to capacity. The place was buzzing and the bar was doing brisk trade. At eight forty-five. Kevo introduced the band and the first piece, '*Satin Doll'*. It went down well and the applause filled '*Swing 'n' Sax'* with confidence. They played another three or four pieces and then had a break. Jim came over to Edna,

'What do you think, then?'

'Marvellous,' she replied. 'I've been listening to what people are saying, they think you're good. They really like what you're playing.'

The second half was even better. People liked the band and could recognise the pieces. Kevo had pitched it just right. At the end of the evening, Kevo surprised the band by telling them that they would be playing there the following month, if they agreed. Of course they did! The crowd at the '*Black Swan*' loved them. Soon, they had a regular monthly slot.

In October it was Edna's birthday. This year it clashed with the band playing at the '*Black Swan*'.

'If you don't want me to go, if you'd rather we did something just the two of us, I'll understand. Just let me know,' Jim said.

'I want you to go,' Edna said, 'I want to come with you. I can't think of a better birthday present.'

Jim was pleased, well, to be honest, Jim was over the moon.

The next week, Jim told the other members of the group that it would be Edna's birthday when they played the '*Black Swan*', he asked if they'd mind doing him a favour.

When Edna and Jim arrived at the pub, Edna sat down. The pub was busy, as usual. The band certainly brought in customers. At eight forty-five, Kevo introduced them and they were off. They started with '*Satin Doll*'. It had become a band tradition. At the interval Jim sat with Edna.

'Enjoying it love?' he asked.

'As always,' Edna replied.

Towards the end of the set, Kevo announced that there was a birthday girl in, the wife of one of the band members. Kevo looked at Edna,

'Come on, Edna, stand up.'

Edna stood while the band and the customers

sang '*Happy Birthday*'.

Kevo looked round the pub and then looked back at Edna.

'We've not finished yet, Edna,' he said.

Then he proceeded to count the band in. It only took a few bars before Edna said, '*Moonlight in Vermont*', oh thank you."

Jim looked across at Edna and winked.

Moonlight in Vermont - Words & Music by John Blackburn & Karl Suessdorf.

3 THE LETTER

'Don't worry, - mum, dad. I can look after myself.'

'You're seventeen, that's all, not a man until twenty-one, remember that. And you're my son and we want you back here on the farm. We're relying on you.'

His father squeezed his wife's hand as he spoke. He was worried but trying not to show it, not to his son anyway. His wife knew that he would be churning up inside and that his words were as much to comfort himself as to comfort his son.

William turned, hugged his mother, shook hands with his father and set off. Turning one last time he surveyed the familiar landscape, '*when would he return*?' he wondered.

His father and mother watched as William became just a dot moving along the road and when he disappeared from view, they went back into the house.

'They'll look after him, won't they?' his mother said.

'Of course they will, they'll have you to deal with if they don't!'

His mother tried to smile but it was all she could do to stop from crying. The months passed. William would be training first at Chester. That brought her some comfort. He wasn't that far away, yet.

His father missed him on the farm and local help was in short supply. Most of the young men had left with William. The older men who were left behind had to get on and help each other. '*War*,' his father thought, '*what a bloody, awful business.*'

'Young William was a good help with the horses, no one like him in the county, I'd say,' Bill Hawkins remarked to William's father one afternoon in the spring of 1916.

'We'll be glad to have him back, that's for certain,' William's father replied, 'and his mother misses him. It's terrible some days.'

William's parents didn't know where their son would be sent. Wherever it was, they felt it would be a contrast to the Cheshire countryside he knew and loved and that was part of him.

Christmas 1916 arrived. Days of heavy snowfall had left the earth covered in white – pure, innocent, untouched.

There was no letter from William. He wasn't good at writing but he'd never left it so long between letters before.

'He wouldn't let Christmas go by without a word,' his mother said.

January 1917. Still no word, until in the early spring of that year a letter arrived. What must it have been like? The father's pain, the mother's grief. Their son was dead. Killed in action, 1st October 1916, part of the British Expeditionary Force to France.

The envelope also contained William's personal effects. His father had to sign the enclosed form and return it at '*his earliest convenience*'. The 'effects' he signed for was one photograph. A photograph of himself and his wife - mum and dad. That was it. That was all that came home.

4 OLD SOLDIERS NEVER DIE

I'm going on a trip today, on the bus. I'll get the first bus that comes along. This shall be my day of adventure. Now, stick, keys, bus pass, we're off!

I see she's at the stop again, in my seat. Why does she choose the middle seat? When I was in the army, recruits looked up to me. Saw me coming and thought there was going to be a thunderstorm. Don't have the same effect now. I'm no one. I'll twirl my walking stick, that'll annoy her.

I'm sitting down now. I'll give it a minute or two and then I'll start my stick twirling. It's warm, I'm glad of the sit down. I can see her watching me, eyes rolling heavenward to register disgust. It can be my game, my game for the day.

I feel the need to yawn, can't get my breath. It wasn't supposed to be like this. Not here, like this. My head is fit to burst. I feel a trickling sensation down the back of my neck, like water. I'm falling. She's shouting, '*are you all right? Do you need help*?'

Bloody stupid question! Of course I need help! She's laying me on the floor. There's no one else around. God help me! Now she's on her 'phone, who's she's calling? I can't hear anything. Just want to sleep. Just want to be left alone.

5 REFLECTIONS OF MURDER

8.55am.

'No news yet, then?' The assistant asked.

'No Karen; nothing. It's been two weeks now and nothing.'

Geoff picked up his cigarettes and milk from the counter and walked out of the shop. He was a tall, dark haired man in his mid thirties. In another era he could have been a matinee idol. In reality he was a freelance journalist and his wife had recently gone missing.

It was the type of story Geoff would've lapped up a few weeks ago. He'd have been at the door of the person concerned before you could spit. He would've had photos as well. He wouldn't have bothered about how the victim's family were feeling. He would've been after the best take on the story he could find. He'd have dug deep to get anything he could on the victim and their family, as well. There was nothing 'dignified' about the job he did, but he did it well. Now, the tables were turned. He was the victim. No one ventured near him or his grief. There was it seemed, honour among thieves.

In Newham, DI Stuart Evans and Sergeant Nick Craig were poring over the notes and information they had received when Mel Ellis was first reported missing by her husband. She'd failed to return from work at the local library. It was a journey she'd made many times. It was a journey that should've taken no more than ten minutes. It was as though she had vanished into thin air. No one had seen her after she had finished work. Her colleagues at the library were struggling to come to terms with what had happened. They'd all been interviewed, but at the moment the police were still in the dark. What could have happened to the friendly, yet quiet girl everyone seemed to like?

10.42am.

The officer at the desk put down the receiver. Turning to her superior she handed him a piece of paper, 'they've found a woman's body sir, in Newham Wood.'

D I Evans, a man in his late forties took the note and went through to his office. He sat down. He wanted to light a cigarette but knew he couldn't. It wasn't done these days. You couldn't smoke in the workplace. There were very few places left where you could smoke. Politics made Evans' blood boil. He had no time for any of these rules that he could see being imposed on people at will. And yet in his job, in his place of work, he dealt with all the grubby scum that was left when people did break the rules, and went for it in a big way. Sergeant Craig followed him through. He was a tall, slim man with blond hair. In his mid thirties, he thought that sergeant was probably as high as he would get on the promotion ladder. He didn't brood over it, and he liked working with Evans, something his predecessors had not. In his office, Evans made all the rules. He didn't like them to be broken. After a brief discussion, Evans and Craig left the station. They headed for the wood. Evans had a feeling that they would find Mel Ellis there. In fact he was sure of it.

'The body was brought here. She was murdered somewhere else,' D I Evans said, 'I'm sure of that. Get the forensics team here, cordon off the area. I don't want anything disturbed.'

Back at the station arrangements were made to keep Geoff Ellis informed of any developments. Sometime later a car would be sent for him. He was needed to identify the body. To make sure that it was Mel Ellis.

Geoff identified the female as his wife, Mel. '*They've taken her but they can never take away what we had. Bastards.*' He kept these thoughts to himself as he walked home. The police tried to offer words of comfort to him. Geoff wasn't in the mood for accepting. He had just found out that his wife had been murdered.

Geoff carried on over the next few days as best he could. It was difficult. Mel's face kept coming into his head. He could see her laughing, blowing him a kiss, dying. Dying, that was the image that was the most difficult to erase. '*Did she suffer?*' he wondered.

Derek Mills was calm when the police paid him a visit. It was not unexpected. After all, he was a friend of the missing woman, a close friend and they worked together in the local library. Derek got on well with Mel. He liked her. He was however a loner, kept himself to himself. It would be difficult for an outsider to even hazard a guess as to what went on in the head of Derek Mills. Evans and Craig wouldn't try to analyse him, not yet.

Derek was a slightly built man of medium height. His hair was blond and professionally highlighted. Perhaps first appearances would suggest that he wasn't your average librarian.

'What do you make of him, Craig?' D I Evans asked.

'Not much, but something doesn't sit right.'

'We'll watch him. Maybe let him know we're watching him.'

Evans and Craig did watch Mills. They didn't know whether he knew. They weren't really bothered whether he knew, but a few days later they paid him another visit.

'Derek, can we come in? We just need to clear a few things up. Get a better picture in our mind,' Sergeant Craig said.

They followed Derek into the front room of his neat, clean house. All the while D I Evans was taking in the environment. He let Craig do most of the talking, and all the while Derek was watching Evans.

‘The evening Mel disappeared, could you tell us your exact movements?’

‘I wasn’t working that day, and I wasn’t sure whether I was needed the following day. There’d been a mix up with the roster and I was hoping for a call from Miss Jackson. The call never came, and so I decided to call in at the library in the evening, to see if it was sorted out. I thought I’d wait and see if Mel was walking home. If Geoff wasn’t waiting for her, I’d walk part way home with her.’

‘You were soft on her, weren’t you,’ D I Evans said.

‘Yes, but she didn’t want anything to do with me, she was married, well you know that,’ he laughed.

‘Carry on,’ Evans said.

‘I waited until Mel came out and then I spoke to her. She waited for Geoff for a while and when he didn’t show I walked as far as the common road with her. I joked as we walked along. She got on to me about that. I think I got on her nerves a bit.’

‘And then?’

‘I wanted to have just one night with her, just one. She wasn’t interested though. I know it was wrong of me but I drugged her and brought her back here.’

‘How did you drug her?’

‘I had a syringe and as I pulled her towards me I used it. It was easy. She woke up a couple of hours later and she was really annoyed with me. I’d never seen this side of her before and I was shocked. She kept saying that Geoff would be worried and what did I think I was doing. She even said I was mad! I didn't care. She was here with me. Mel was in my house! I loved her you see. I really loved her. I don't think Geoff did. No one could love Mel like I did. It was special, total. Nothing else mattered.'

'Did you kill her?

'No. I've told you, I loved Mel. I just wanted her with me, just for a little while. I just wanted her to be here with me.'

'Did you sleep with her?'

'No. I would never do that. I loved her too much. Mel was special.'

'Where did you get the drugs, what did you use?'

'I don't know what it was, the bloke I got the stuff from told me what to do, said it would work.'

'Where did you get the drugs?'

'Down at the dog track. I'd met up with a bloke there. Earlier in the week I'd been in the pub and asked around. The whole thing was easier than I thought.'

'The names of these blokes?'

'I don't know, sorry.'

'I bet you are. When did she leave?'

'I took her home just after eleven o'clock. She'd come round a bit then and was getting rather loud. I didn't like it. I walked her to her door and watched her go into the house.'

'And that's it?'Craig asked.

'That's it. She was quite alive when I left her. I swear it.'

'You know we're going to have to take you to the station. We need you to make a statement there and you'll be charged,' Evans said.

'I know. But I didn't kill her.'

Derek was taken to the police station and given over to the duty staff. Evans and Craig would get back to him later.

'What do you think sir, did he do it?'

'No.'

'Any ideas?'

'Plenty.'

Geoff Ellis had a visit from Evans and Craig that same day.

'Mrs Bruce your mother-in-law, do you get on with her?'

'Never met her, so I don't know. Mel used to keep in touch but I hardly spoke really, except maybe Christmas morning. Mel would put me on Skype with instructions-'wish mum a happy Christmas'. I don't think Mel's mum was too pleased that we married here. I think they would have preferred it to take place in New Zealand. Mel's from a place called Waikiri, near Canterbury, but Mel didn't want that. She hated fuss.

Anyway, we married here and since then I think I've been seen as the 'bad guy'.'

'Where were you on the evening of your wife's disappearance?'

'We've been through all this before. I've told you, I was here waiting for Mel to return from work.'

'You didn't go out looking for her when she was late? After all it is only a short walk from your home to the library.'

'No, not right away.'

'Not right away. When did you go then?'

'About nine-fifteen.'

'And where did you go, where did you go to look for your wife Mr Ellis?'

'I walked to the end of the common road.'

'Was there anyone else there?'

'No.'

'Did you see any cars or did anyone else pass you on the route?'

'No.'

'So you were totally alone?'

'Yes.'

'Did you love your wife Mr Ellis?'

'Yes. Of course I did.'

Geoff started to fidget. Evans and Craig could see he was uneasy but they needed to keep chipping away. If they did, they felt he might break.

'You know we have Derek Mills in custody?' Evans said.

'Yes. How's it going with him, you know he had a thing about Mel, don't you? He was infatuated with her. Worshipped the ground she walked on.'

'I'm afraid I'm not at liberty to answer your question but I can tell you that we're making progress. I'm surprised to learn from you that they were quite so close. I thought they were merely 'work colleagues'. But there are some more questions we'd like to ask you, if that's all right?'

'It's fine with me. I just want whoever it was, whoever was responsible for what happened to Mel ... I want them caught.'

'That's what we'd all like Mr Ellis, now if we can carry on. Did you know Mr Mills at all?'

'No, well only in passing. I'd seen him when I'd met Mel from work. He'd been at the library three or four months. I just passed the time of day with him sometimes while I was waiting for Mel. Just hello, goodbye and chat about the weather, that type of thing.'

'Did Mel speak of him at all?'

'Not really. She thought he was a loner, a bit sad – but Mel being Mel she'd be a friend to anyone.'

'Right, and this friendship he shared with your wife. What can you tell us about that?'

'Not a great lot. I only know what Mel told me. He was always wanting to help her at the library, and if I wasn't there to meet Mel, he would appear, to the rescue as it were. I mean, you've seen him. Looks a bit of a wimp to me; can't quite imagine him as the knight in shining armour, can you? To be honest, all that I know for sure was that he got on Mel's nerves. If he wasn't helping her or turning up to walk her home he was telling stupid jokes or playing pranks.'

'That will be all for the time being. We'll be back in touch, but for the moment that's it. Thanks Mr Ellis, we'll see ourselves out.'

Helen Bruce arrived in Newham early in the morning after an overnight flight. Her sister Jean was travelling with her. There hadn't been a need for her to come half way around the world, of course. The police in New Zealand could relay any news of her daughter's disappearance to her, and they had. But now her daughter had been found, she felt a need to be with her, to see her one last time. The flight hadn't been the easiest to undertake and the circumstances of her visit left her feeling drained. She didn't really want to be interviewed, but now she was here...and in a house provided by the police. How could she have anticipated this episode in her life? And, more to the point, she had to do it all alone. Her sister had accompanied her, but a sister isn't your husband.

Mel's father had died three years earlier and Helen felt the new burden of her daughter's death intolerable*, 'What could've happened for her daughter to have come to her end in this way? Everything was so 'odd'.*

It had been arranged that Evans and Craig would meet Mrs Bruce the following day, a policewoman would accompany them. It sometimes helped in these situations to have a female on the team.

Mrs Bruce and her sister had flown in from New Zealand. A house had been arranged for them to stay in, a house away from prying eyes and insensitive journalists. Evans insisted that everything be as normal as possible within the restrictions he had laid down.

It was obvious when they met with Mrs Bruce that she had been crying. Her eyes were red rimmed and puffy. She was a small lady, grey haired and she wore glasses which seemed too big for her face. Evans and Craig could see that the interview would be an ordeal for her. Jean was younger and looked to be of a stronger constitution. Evans was glad that she was there. It would help ease the pressure.

'How long had your daughter known Geoff before the marriage took place?' Sergeant Craig asked.

'Two, maybe three months. Not long at all. You can't know someone after only three months. You can't.'

'Did you come to England for the wedding?'

'No. This was the cause of another upset. Her father doted on her, but he was too ill to travel. He wanted her to come home to marry, just so he could see her and meet Geoff, and, and give her away, but no, it didn't happen and John died six weeks later.'

'I'm sorry to hear that. What had the contact with your daughter been like since her marriage, have you visited?'

'Not much contact really, perhaps a 'phone call once a month. I haven't visited nor have they been over to New Zealand. Mel didn't even come home for her dad's funeral. That hurt. That really hurt but Mel seemed happy and so I had to be satisfied with that. I was due to visit her, to visit them, in June for Mel's birthday. She would have been thirty but that's all done now, too.'

'I won't take up much more of your time Mrs Bruce, but I do need to ask just one or two more questions, if that's all right'

'I know you have to ask, really I'll be fine,' but then as she spoke she squeezed the arm of the policewoman who was sitting next to her, as if for comfort. She was a shattered human being.

'When did Mel settle in England?'

'When she was twenty. She visited for the first time when she was eighteen and when she returned home her father and I knew we'd lost her. She loved it here and all she wanted to do was to save and then come back over to live.'

'So she was here about five or six years before she married?'

'Yes.'

'Any other boyfriends that you know of Mrs Bruce, before she married Geoff?'

'No, I don't think so. She had friends, work colleagues from the library, but that's all they were, friends. As far as I know there was no one special until Geoff.'

'Have you spoken to Geoff since Mel's disappearance?'

'No. It was always Mel who rang so there was nothing wrong as far as I knew, not until I was contacted by the police. So as far as Geoff is concerned I haven't had any contact at all.'

'So you've never met him?'

'No. Odd isn't it? I have photographs of course, but no, I've never met him.'

Back at the station Evans was collecting his thoughts. Craig had gone to interview Lynn Davis, another work colleague of Mel's. When he returned there wasn't much to add to what they had found out so far, from Geoff and from Helen Bruce.

They knew Lynn and Mel were friends and that Lynn found Derek odd and had warned her about him and his, what she thought to be, obsessive behaviour.

There was another link between these people, there must be. There must be something they were missing. Evans sat at his desk, thoughts tumbling through his head. Mel had been stabbed through the heart. That was how she had met her end but as yet no murder weapon had been found. She had been drugged as well, but they believed Derek Mills' story to be true. He had drugged her but not killed her. The person she went home to that night was Geoff. '*Geoff Ellis, there has to be more to that man than we know. We've just got to bring it to the surface.*'

Evans sat quietly. This case was awkward. The pieces didn't fit neatly together.

Sergeant Craig went to see Mrs Bruce alone. Evans was still at his desk going through all the paperwork. He knew he was missing something. He hoped that this elusive 'something' would suddenly jump out and hit him.

'*She looks more rested today,*' Craig thought as he walked into the room where Mrs Bruce was sitting.

'Did your daughter ever mention anyone at all to you that she may have been friendly with? I'm including female friends in this.'

'No, not really. I only know Lynn from the library. When Mel first came to England she and Lynn shared a house together.'

'How did that come about? Had they known each other before Mel moved here?'

'No. I think they met at work. Yes they did. I'm

sure that's what Mel said.'

'At the library?'

'No. When Mel first came here, to England, she lived in Southport. She took a summer job at the theatre. Lynn was already working there. They became fast friends, but Lynn was always more outgoing. I think that's maybe why they got on so well. Even as a child Mel was always shy, very quiet. You know sergeant, I wish you could've met her when she was alive, got to talk to her. She was quiet but yet everyone seemed to like her. She hadn't a nasty bone in her body, she would befriend anyone. I can picture her now, her dark hair tumbling over her shoulders. She had lovely hair, naturally wavy, too. A lot of people would pay for that. Mel didn't have to, she already had it. It was a gift.'

Craig smiled. '*Every mother loves her children.'*

'Did you ever meet Lynn?'

'Yes. The year after Mel emigrated they came over to New Zealand together. Mel had been offered a job at Newham library. She wasn't going to be starting until the October, so she decided to use up some free time and visit home.'

'What did you think of Lynn?'

'She seemed a genuinely nice girl. She always had a tale to tell or a funny story, usually about some or other scrape that she'd been in, now whether they were true or not, these tales, I don't know, but what I do know is that there was no harm in her. Yes, Lynn was a good sort. She got on well with all of us'

'You say Lynn got on well with all of you. Who did that include?'

'Oh, I'm sorry for not making myself clear, sergeant. I meant only to include the three of us, me, Mel and her father.' Helen Bruce turned and looked at her sister who was sitting impassively on the sofa.

'You never met Lynn, did you Jean?'

Jean looked straight at Craig before replying,

'No. I don't think I did.' Craig smiled at Jean and carried on,

'Did Lynn already work at the library when Mel was offered her job there?'

'No. Lynn carried on working at the theatre. It wasn't until the following March, after Mel had worked at the library for about six months that another vacancy occurred. Mel suggested to Lynn that she apply. I think Mel was a little lonely in Newham. New job, new flat, not many friends. At that time Mel was the youngster in the library, by her own account all the other staff were 'oldies'.'

'Did Lynn know Geoff?'

'I don't think so.'

'How did Mel and Geoff meet?'

' I'm not sure, but Mel 'phoned one day and she was so happy. Even on the 'phone I could tell that there was a new happiness in her voice. She was gushing over this boy she had just met. That her father was terminally ill didn't seem to matter, and they had always been so close. It was so very, very sad.'

'But you were happy for your daughter?'

'Reservedly so, yes. Remember sergeant, I had

not and still haven't met Geoff Ellis.'

'Do you know where they met initially, did they know each other socially perhaps?'

'You'd have to ask Geoff that question. I'm afraid I don't know. It was never discussed.'

'Do you think your daughter made a mistake?'

'A mistake?'

'A mistake in her choice of man?'

'Every mother would probably hope for someone different as a son in law, no matter how good their daughter's choice, but as I have just said I never met Geoff, and I still haven't met him so I'm afraid I can't answer that, sergeant.'

Jean, who had been sitting silently in the room up to this point, turned and looked at her sister.

'Tea?' she asked.

'That would be nice,' Helen replied, 'Sergeant, would you join us?'

Derek Mills was kept in custody for forty-eight hours. An application was in hand to extend the length of time they could detain him. Evans was hoping he got authority in time and didn't have to release him. They couldn't charge him with Mel's murder; they hadn't enough to go on, not yet. If the worst came to the worse he could be charged with kidnap, but there again, even when charged he could be released on bail. Lawyers could be canny animals. Evans was pondering all these things. '*Was it that he was getting old?*'

At the library the staff carried on, albeit under a cloud. A lot of people in the town knew Mel and were obviously saddened by her death. Lynn however, had difficulty coping with those customers who came into the library and wanted to 'chat' about Mel. She was moved to tears many times by their insensitivity and blatant curiosity. These people who she saw week upon week were now fixated by the latest gossip. Gossip, that was what Mel had become.

'You look as though you've had enough,' Angie Evans said as her husband came through the door.

'Mmm, just don't ask. When do we eat?'

'About ten minutes.'

Angie carried on with the task of preparing the evening meal. She knew better than to talk to him when he was like this. Dinner was a quiet affair. Angie didn't ask. Stuart Evans was tight lipped. Angie didn't like it. She knew from past experience that 'awkward' cases took their toll on their relationship. He wouldn't let her in. Emotional support was probably the only way she could help but Stuart always kept her out, wouldn't let her share the burden. This made her feel isolated from him, and in their twenty years of marriage it wasn't getting any easier. It was still difficult to manage. She'd left him once, briefly, just after their fifth anniversary. The break up lasted a few months. They couldn't seem to live together or to survive apart. It was tough. They decided a truce was the only way to get back together. It had remained like that ever since. Their love for each other was never in doubt. That was for keeps, whatever.

Angie washed up the dinner things. Stuart came into the kitchen. He smiled. *'He looks young when he smiles'. 'Just like when we first met'.*

'What are you thinking?' he asked.

'Me, nothing, oh well if you must know, I'm thinking, I love you Stuart Evans.'

Evans was a little late in the following morning. He looked awful. Craig remarked on it.

'Thanks', Evans replied, 'I needed that.'

'I've found a little nugget about Ellis, sir, if you're interested.'

'Go on.'

'Before he was freelance he used to work as a journalist for the local paper in Malverton. He didn't have many friends. In fact he made far more enemies. He, as my mother would say 'embroidered' a lot – you know, not much of a story, add to it, embellish it. By the time it reaches the papers no one's sure what's right anymore.'

'Aren't all papers like that?'

'OK. But Ellis over egged the pudding. And that's not all. There's an ex. A Mrs Ellis number one. She still lives in Malverton and I'm off to see her this afternoon, two o'clock. They met while they were both working on the local paper in Malverton, 'The Echo'. She was an office junior and only seventeen when they met. They married within the year. Her parents weren't too pleased, thought she was too young.'

'How do you know all this?'

'Mrs Ellis number one has a mother, she 'phoned in last night.'

'Carry on, Craig.'

Craig returned just after five pm. Evans was still at his desk.

'Anything new?' he asked as Craig walked through the door.

'Plenty, you might like to listen to this. Ellis married Annie Gibbons five years ago.'

'Her mother told me that she was glad her daughter hadn't 'had to get married' you know sir, being so young, but the fact of the matter is the marriage only lasted six months and then it was annulled. You see sir, it was never consummated. Miss Gibbons intimated that she had doubts about Geoff after the first few weeks, especially as nothing had happened, as it were. She thought he may have had 'male friends'. Incidentally, she's passed on some photographs. They'll need to be enhanced but some of them are possibly quite interesting.'

'Did Annie Gibbons mention Derek Mills to you, does she know him?'

'No, that's the interesting bit. I've arranged to go back and see her, after the lab's played around with the photos for us.' He passed the prints to Evans.

'You see sir, I bet any money that chap at the back is Mills. Annie Gibbons referred to him as Keith Davies.'

Evans at once became more interested, 'you'd better get on to it then, hadn't you!'

At the library things were beginning to get back

to some sort of normality. Staff had been brought in to cover for those missing and two vacancies had been advertised.

The next morning Craig was despatched to see Mrs Bruce. Evans had a feeling she might be holding something back. He thought it would be easier for Craig to try and fathom it on his own.

When he arrived back, it was to an office in turmoil. Evans had been going through everything, trying to find the missing piece. He looked up as he caught sight of Craig approaching,

'Have you learnt anything from your visit today?'

'Not much, sir. Just more background details. What about you?'

'No, but it's here somewhere, I know it is. The problem is I just can't see it.'

Craig passed his notes across to DI. Evans.

'What's this, Craig?'

'What?'

'This piece at the bottom about 'wills'?'

'Oh that. Mel Ellis was quite a wealthy woman. Her father, when he died had left her $1,000,000 New Zealand dollars.'

'And we know he died six weeks after Mel married Geoff. Geoff knew before he married her that her father was terminally ill. She was an only child. This could be it Craig. We need to do more background on Geoff Ellis. Derek Mills, I bet he knows more about Geoff than he's letting on.'

Evans was at full tilt the next morning.

'We need to speak to Ellis, Mrs Bruce and

Derek Mills. Derek Mills is probably holding the key to this whole affair. Oh, and Lynn, the library assistant, we need to talk to her again. I bet there's something she's withholding because she thinks it's irrelevant, doesn't believe it's important, we'll check the library first.'

Craig went into the library to talk to Lynn. Evans wandered about among the shelves. He was a great believer in just 'watching'.

'Lynn. Thanks for taking the time out to talk again. I just need to go over some details again. It shouldn't take very long. Did you know Geoff Ellis before he met and married Mel?'

'No. I don't know where she met him. You see Mel and I shared a flat together, so you would've thought we'd have been quite close. I even went out to New Zealand with her to visit, stayed with her parents. They were very nice and made me welcome, which under the circumstances was so good of them, I mean Mel's father was ill and I'd just dropped in out of the blue really but they were really good to me. But, having said all that we weren't 'close'. We were really good friends and that was it. Mel was very insular and didn't confide in me or tell me much really about her private life. With Mel there was always a part that you felt was never open to you. She always seemed to be holding something back.'

'Derek Mills, apart from working with him in the library did you know him.'

'No. Until he started work here we'd never met.'

'Did Mel ever make any mention of a legacy

she might have inherited?'

Lynn laughed. 'Do you mean the $1,000,000?'

'Yes.'

'There never was any will. Mel laughed about it when she told me. There should've been but Mel's dad was so ill all the money was used to pay hospital bills and doctor's fees. What was left is still in Mel's mum's account. They weren't a 'wealthy' family. That money was all their life savings. Mel would never have seen her own mother destitute. Mel even paid something each month into her mother's account from her salary at the library.'

'But her mother's under the impression that her husband left the money to Mel.'

'That's what Mel wanted her to think. She thinks the library cheque is a monthly premium from her husband's estate. Mel was kind. She was the sort of person who would befriend anyone, help anyone. I daresay though, that her mother will soon realise what was going on when the 'monthly premiums' stop.'

'Mr Ellis, may we come in? We'll be brief, I promise,' Craig waited for a reply. Evans smiled. The look was one of a certain endearment, although Geoff Ellis knew it meant nothing.

'Yes, come in,' he replied.

Craig continued,

'We're concerned that Mr. Mills may have had an accomplice. Did Mel ever mention to you anyone else she'd seen with Mr. Mills, either at work or socially? Or perhaps someone he'd mentioned to her, a friend from the past, perhaps?'

'No. I don't think he had any friends. I told you before, Mel said he was a loner.'

'Had you or your wife made a will?'

'No. Never thought of it. You don't when you're young, do you?'

'Bank accounts, did you have a joint account or separate accounts?'

'Why?'

'We have to get a picture of you Mr Ellis. You'd be surprised how little ordinary things can be of significant help. You might not think so, but to us it can be the missing piece of the jigsaw. We will find your wife's killer, Mr Ellis. Of that I'm certain.'

Evans made a mental note that Ellis didn't seem to take any solace from the last statement. In fact it seemed to make his attitude more tense and abrasive. His response was terse.

'Fine. We had a joint account, and Mel had an account of her own. The accounts, they're with Shaws in Newham High Street.'

'Thank you. When Mel's father died, did you receive anything, a legacy?'

'No.'

'No?' Evans replied, involuntarily. Ellis looked at him, Evans turned and Craig carried on.

'Did you have any money worries, Mr Ellis?'

'No, none. I work freelance as a writer. I get paid well for what I do. Mel's salary at the library wasn't fantastic, but neither did we need her to work. She worked at the library because she liked it, nothing more.'

Evans was still struggling with his lapse of concentration.

'What was the matter with him?' Evans knew he should be under more control than this. This case was getting to him.

He cleared his mind and could hear Craig talking somewhere. It seemed as if he was speaking through a haze. It was a good job they would soon be on their way. Evans needed to get outside, to breathe in some fresh air.

'Are you all right, Sir?' Craig asked as they left the house and headed for the car.

'I wish I knew,' Evans replied.

The next day Craig was despatched to interview Mills again, he was still in custody but his lawyers had applied for bail.

There wasn't enough evidence to charge him with Mel's murder but he had been charged with kidnap. The bail was granted, much to Evans' annoyance.

'Who's standing surety for him?' Craig asked.

'His mother.'

'She's come out of the woodwork. Where does this 'mother' live?'

'In Chedbackston. By the old manor. She actually lives in the lodge.'

'I'll be paying her a visit then?'

'First thing in the morning.'

The next morning Nick Craig was busy. He was going to see Mills' mother at ten-thirty, also he'd arranged to meet with Lynn again in the afternoon, at her home.

'Nice home you have here,' Craig said as he entered the lodge that was home to Derek Mills' mother.

'Thank you,' she said. 'Do sit down. We bought it when my husband was alive. He seemed to like the fact that it was quite a salubrious address. I just liked it, but I'm sure you've not come all the way out here to chat about homes and interior design. You want to know about Derek?'

Mills mother was a typical 1950's mum. She seemed trapped in an ideal of the past. Her hair was grey now, but still 'set'. Craig imagined that she would have a weekly visit to the hairdresser. It was probably the highlight of her week. She was smartly and neatly dressed, and at her throat, a string of pearls.

'Sergeant, are you all right, you seem to have drifted off?'

'I'm fine thanks. We'll carry on now.'

'Would you like some tea, perhaps, before we start?'

'Thank you. That would be nice.'

Craig sat in the comfortable sitting room and waited for Mrs Mills to return. She didn't take long.

'I'd already set things up,' she said, 'in anticipation. Now please, carry on.'

'You've stood bail for your son. You know he's been arrested in connection with the kidnap of Melanie Ellis, a work colleague?'

'Yes, but he's also my son. What mother would do anything different?'

'He doesn't live here with you at all, perhaps stay over sometimes?'

'No. He's an adult sergeant, he has his own life to live and I wouldn't want it any other way. Do you live with your parents?'

'No.'

'And are you married or single?'

'Single.'

'You have your answer then.'

'You know he's said he was in love with her?'

'I don't. But she was a married woman, or so I believe. I don't think you really know anything about my son.' Mrs Mills laughed. 'I think you'll have to come up with something a little better than that, sergeant. If you're trying to shock me, it isn't going to work.'

'I'm not trying to shock you, just get answers to some questions. Did you ever meet Melanie Ellis, did you ever visit the library in Newham?'

'I'm sorry I can't help you. I didn't know her at all and I never visit libraries.'

Craig took a card from his jacket pocket and handed it to Mrs Mills.

'That's the number for the station. If you think of anything that may help us, just call.'

Craig left Mrs Mills on her own. He never did drink his tea.

Evans sat at his desk and tried in vain to get things clear in his mind. He needed to understand why he was finding this case difficult to deal with. Awkward cases meant more pressure. He knew that.

And however difficult he could usually see his way through and get on with things. *'What was making this one so difficult?'*

When Craig returned, it was to find that Mills had been released. His lawyer had come for him and driven him home.

'What did you get from his mother?' Evans asked.

'Precisely nothing.' Craig replied.

'Well, don't sit there, go and see him, see if he lets go of any little nuggets that might be useful to us, and don't forget, you're going round to see Lynn Davies this afternoon.'

'No rest for the wicked, eh?'

'You've got it in one,' Evans replied.

Craig didn't like Mills much and felt that he wasn't being straight with him but he battled on regardless, trying to make a dint in the wall that Mills had so skilfully put up.

'Mr. Mills, I feel like this isn't getting me anywhere and I don't know why. I feel as though there's a lot more you could be saying. You might not know that you're missing out details. I believe you think you are answering as fully as possible, so, don't worry, however, I've some notes here that I'll refer to as we go along'

Derek laughed, 'He's always struck me as a bit of a tyrant, your boss, he's the one who's set you up with notes, isn't he?'

'We'd better just get straight on with the interview.' Craig then referred to his notes and began questioning Mills.

He found it irritating, irritating even being in the same room with him, but it had to be done.

'You loved Mel, didn't you?'

'Yes.'

'You couldn't have killed her, then. Maybe someone wanted you to kill her and you tried, but because you loved her you just couldn't go through with it, is that how it was?'

'I've told you, I didn't kill her. I loved her. I would never hurt Mel.'

'But you said you drugged her. Wasn't that hurting her? Hardly the way someone in love would behave?'

'I can't remember.'

'Or don't want to remember?'

'I don't know.'

'This isn't helping us, is it?'

'I'm trying. Ask me something that I can answer.'

'Ok. Did Geoff love Mel?'

'He said he did.'

'What do you think, Derek?'

'I don't know. He should've done. She was very beautiful, and kind. I loved her.'

'How did you find out about the job at the library, Derek?'

'It was advertised in the paper.'

'You'd worked in a library before, hadn't you?'

'Yes.'

'Where was that?'

'Malverton.'

'Malverton's only twelve miles from here. Are

you sure you never met Geoff Ellis before you moved to Newham and took the job at the library?'

'Yes. I'm sure.'

The next day Evans said he would accompany Craig. It was planned to interview Mel's mother, Mrs Bruce, again. When they walked in, it was obvious to see that Helen Bruce had been crying. Evans felt a sickness fill the pit of his stomach, '*was he getting past it, was all this dealing with other people's grief becoming too much for him?*'

He thought that maybe it was. Helen's sister sat with her and tried to comfort her.

'We're trying to make funeral arrangements, but everything is impossible at the moment. We don't know when we can have her back you see, no one is forthcoming, so we try and think of the things we can arrange, like making sure her favourite music is played, that all the family will be able to attend and the form the service will take.'

'Are you expecting to have your daughter taken back to New Zealand? Is that why you're making plans for the service?' Evans asked.

'I don't see any reason why not,' Helen Bruce replied.

'Have you spoken to Mr Ellis about any of this? You see as her husband, he is next of kin,' Evans asked.

'No.' Mrs Bruce stated quite definitely, 'but Mel was my daughter for nearly thirty years. Her husband had known her for less than three. I think that gives me the right.'

‘Mrs Bruce, if you need any counselling or help with any arrangements once everything can go ahead, we do have people who can help you,’ was Evans next offering.

‘There’s no need, I’ll arrange things myself. I have a good family.’ Helen glanced up at her sister.

Jean smiled.

Craig continued, ‘Have you any photos of Geoff and Mel that we could borrow? Just for a few days.’

‘Why?’ Helen asked.

‘We may see on them other people who may be able to help us with our investigation.’

‘I thought Mr. Mills was the suspect. Do you think there are more?’ Helen answered.

‘We don’t know. That’s the truth of it. But anything that could help us find out what happened to your daughter, that’s what we need, Mrs Bruce.’

‘Most things like that are at home in New Zealand, but I have one or two with me that you can look at. I’m not certain whether there’s anyone else on them though.’

Craig took the photos and thanked Mrs Bruce. Helen’s sister showed them to the door.

‘My sister is beginning to get a little flustered by everything. Please forgive her manner, but I think that given the circumstances it’s understandable.’

‘We’re very sorry, but you do understand that we have a job to do and that it can be difficult at times, for all concerned. We are only trying to help and if you think that your sister would benefit from seeing one of our counsellors, I can set it up.’

Evans truly did want to help and felt that Mrs Bruce had suffered trauma enough.

'I think that would be a good idea,' Jean replied, 'but my sister mustn't know you've arranged it, just let the counsellor drop in sometime. I think that would be best.'

The following morning, Evans and Craig drove the twelve miles to Malverton. They had some photographs to show to Annie Gibbons.

The photographs from Mrs Bruce weren't any help. Annie Gibbons didn't recognise Mel. The ones from Annie Gibbons were a different matter. On several of them there was a young Derek Mills in the background.

'She said the chap in the background was Keith Davies. He was Geoff's best man when they got married,' Craig said.

'And she's telling the truth. He probably wasn't Derek Mills then. I don't think she's anything to hide. On our prints, from the station, he looks a different man. For one thing his blond hair has been highlighted, and he's a little bit older. When she compares the two, when Annie sees these, she'll be able to confirm what we think we already know. She'll remember.'

Annie was expecting them and was ready when Evans and Craig arrived.

'We've blown up and enhanced the photographs you gave us, would you mind having another look at them?' Craig asked.

Craig passed the photos to Annie and then continued, 'Do you know this man? He pointed To Mills. He's on four of the photos you passed on to us.'

'Yes. Of course I know him. That's Keith Davies. He was the best man at our wedding. He and Geoff were always together, '*best mates'*.' Evans produced the prints they had, the more recent ones, and handed them to Annie.

'Now do you know this man?' Evans asked.

'I wouldn't like to say for definite, but I can see there's a likeness between Keith on my photos and the man here.'

Evans spoke again, 'Annie, why did you hang on to the photos of Geoff and Keith, It's none of my business, but it just seems strange?'

'I guess I'll always be in love with him. I'm only twenty-four now, but then I was seventeen. Geoff swept me off my feet. He was my first love. First love is always special. I thought you'd have known that.'

'That's the link then,' Evans said to Craig as they drove back to Newham. I bet Mills/Davies, whatever he called himself, I bet he and Geoff Ellis were lovers. They probably split up and Geoff married shy, little Mel on the rebound.'

'What about Annie? Geoff was married to her first.'

'I know, but that marriage was never consummated. I don't know why Ellis married Annie. I would think at the time he was still having his fling with Mills. It was probably after the divorce that Geoff and Mills split up. Probably got fed up with each other, or Geoff became tired of Mills. I would imagine Ellis was the senior partner in this. What he said, well that was it. Mills had to obey.'

'Why do you think it happened? That they got together again? He did seem happy with Mel, by all accounts.'

'I genuinely think that Ellis wanted his marriage to Mel to work. I think that for a time he was in love with her. Mills was the one who put the end to it. He saw the job advertisement for the library at Newham. He'd worked in the library at Malverton and he was a good librarian, we know that. They gave him extremely good references and what do you know! He landed the job. His good luck wasn't so good for Mel though. Her number was up almost as soon as Derek started work there. Derek had never really got over Geoff. He knew Geoff had re-married and was living in Newham. I don't think he knew he'd be so lucky as to end up working where he could have contact with him so easily though, that was just fate. And we know that Mel was kind and generous and made friends with the underdog. She probably took Derek under her wing and led him to Geoff. How lucky could Derek get? And we also know that Geoff used to wait and walk home with Mel if she did the late shift at the library. Everything fell into Derek's lap. Once he'd seen Geoff again I assume an affair started. Mel's days were numbered.'

'But you said Ellis loved Mel and he was the stronger partner. Couldn't he just dictate that Mills left his job and move on?'

'You can't always know how someone in love will react. I guess that Ellis had to decide who he was in love with more, and Mel lost. That's all there is to it.'

'I'll need to go and see Mills tomorrow then?' Craig said.

'I'll be joining you,' Evans replied, 'I want to be there when we show him the photographs.'

'Derek Mills, we'd like to come in. I've some photographs we'd like you to have a look at,' Craig announced.

'Come in. I'll help if I can. You know that.'

Evans and Craig followed Mills into the neat, terraced house. Once inside Mills showed them into the small lounge, and offered them a seat.

Craig took the photographs from his pocket and handed them to Mills.

'It's the man at the back, the one we've circled. We wondered if you could identify him? We know Geoff Ellis is on there but we're particularly interested in the other man. Any ideas.'

Mills took the photographs and studied it. Studied it almost too long but at last he said,

'It's me.'

'Would you like to tell us more?' Craig asked.

'I did love Mel,' he said. 'I wanted us to go away together, but you see she really did love Geoff. Trouble was, as you've perhaps gathered by now, I guess you could say Geoff loved me. It would have been all fine if I hadn't taken the job at Newham library. Geoff and Mel would have been ok. I guess I screwed it up for them.'

'You needn't have gone through with it,' Craig replied.

‘I had no choice. I was bound by what had gone before.’

‘You were lovers?’ Craig asked.

‘Yes, but I was young when we first met. I was just eighteen. I ... well it’s no use now, Mel’s dead. Excuses don’t matter.’

‘Did Geoff Ellis have anything to do with the death of his wife?’ Evans asked.

‘Yes, yes. After I drugged her. I was supposed to kill her but I couldn’t. I did love her. If only she had trusted me, she could still be alive.’

‘She trusted her husband, and that didn’t do her any good,’ Evans said.

‘No, I know but’... Derek stopped.

‘Would you like to tell us any more about Keith Davies? That’s a name we know you’re familiar with.’ Craig said.

‘You must’ve spoken to Annie. She’s the only one, apart from Geoff and one or two ‘dalliances’ who knew me as that. So, what can I tell you? I was baptised Derek Mills, on the 30th September 1978, St. Bede’s, Wassington. But again, you know that because you’ll have checked. Keith Davies was the name I used in the early days, when I used to have my little ‘flings’. I’m past all that now. I’ve grown up, or something. There’s no more to tell, but you’ll know that as well.’

‘Have you ever been in trouble with the police before, Mr Mills?’

‘No. And you know that’s the truth.’ Derek grinned, ‘well, what are we waiting for, officers?’

‘You know what comes next?’ Evans said.

‘Yes,’ Mills replied.

When they arrived back at the station Mills was with them. He was taken into custody. Evans didn't want to let him go so easily again. In their last interview he had placed himself with Mel. He had said that Ellis wanted him to murder his wife. This time there wouldn't be any bail.

The next two to have a visit would be Geoff Ellis and Lynn Davies. Lynn was working in the library when Craig called in.

'Is there anywhere we can go out of the public eye?' Craig asked as he approached the desk where Lynn was working.

'Sure, I'll just get another member of staff to cover for me and then we can go to the staff room. It should be quiet there now, all the breaks are finished. I won't be a minute.'

Within a few minutes Lynn was back.

'It's fine, come with me. My manager says we can use her office.'

When they'd gone up to the manager's office, Lynn wasn't as bright as she'd been earlier. Craig could tell that she was dreading the questioning.

'Would you like a cuppa?' Lynn asked.

'No thanks. You get one for yourself, I'll just get on with the questions,' Craig replied.

Lynn made herself a mug of tea and then sat down.

'I think I'll be able to concentrate more easily with this,' she said.

Craig continued, 'I just want to ask you about your friendship with Mel. How was it affected by Derek starting work in the library? He seemed to have a bit of a crush on her.'

'Yes he did. It was terrible. I think he was infatuated with her, even though she was married, and she made that clear to Derek. Once when we were in the back office cataloguing books I tried to broach the subject with her. I told her that I knew we'd known each other for ages but I was still finding it difficult to get the words to come out. I told her I was worried about her. She just said to me, '*ooh, this sounds interesting, carry on, I'm listening.*' I told her that I was bothered about the way that Derek had latched on to her, that she should watch out. I told her he was odd. I told her that I knew she liked taking in strays and befriending everybody but that she should be careful with Derek. I didn't think she should trust him. She just replied, '*Awh, that's nice Lynn, looking out for me. Thank you but I'm handling Derek in my own way.* She said, '*I told him last week that we're just work colleagues, nothing more. I'm beginning to think that I'm getting through to him at last*'. She wasn't though. All he could talk about while I was working with him that afternoon was Mel. He really gave me the creeps. Mel agreed that she was uneasy working with him, but just laughed it off. I tried to get Mel to '*The Bull*', the pub around the corner from the library, for lunch. Before she was married we'd go on a regular basis, once she was married to Geoff though, everything changed. '*The Bull*' was the kind of place that was trapped in time. They still serve '*steak Canadienne*' can you believe that? Mel and I would laugh and say '*if that wasn't on the menu, what would we have?'* I remember the last time we went for lunch there. She was really chirpy. I asked her how Geoff was, she said, *'he's fine – extremely fine'.* She was just so happy.'

'When was that?'

'I can't remember the exact date. I just remember it because it was the last time we went there. If I had to say, probably about three or four months ago.'

'Tell me more about Mills. Do you think he enjoyed his work? Could he have had ulterior motives for being here?'

'This all sounds rather deep,' Lynn replied, and then to Craig's surprise added, 'It's Geoff, isn't it? Geoff's involved. I knew it.'

'We just need to find out all we can about the people closest to Mel. You were not only a friend but a work colleague so, it seems you might know quite a lot about Mel without actually realising it. Just relating conversations that took place can be of so much help'

'I see. There was this one time I was working with Derek on the desk, the reserved items desk and Mel was replacing returned books to the shelves, she was very quiet. Not her usual chatty self. That's a bit of a contradiction in terms, really. Mel was really quiet, kept her own personal thoughts to herself, and then there was another side that was chatty and friendly. She would talk about anything of general interest really, TV from last night, newspaper headlines. She was almost as bad as my mother for getting worked up about the reporting in the '*Daily Mail'*! But to get back to what's really important, on this particular day I had noticed she was really quiet. I had asked her earlier in the day if she was all right. She just said '*yes*' but no more, but as I've told you she didn't talk at all about her private life.'

'Carry on, you were going to mention Mills.'

'Well, he just remarked that she was very quiet, then he said, *'you're her friend aren't you?'* I thought it was a funny thing to say, and I said so. Then he said, '*you are though, aren't you, her friend?*' I said that '*yes I was'.*'

'And?' Craig queried.

He said, '*do you think she likes me?*'

'I was dumfounded. I couldn't believe what he'd just asked.'

'I just replied and said that yes, she probably did like him but that Mel was friends with everybody, that I'd never known one person that she hadn't got on with.'

'What did he say?'

'He said, '*ok. Lynn, you know what I mean. Has she mentioned me to you, you know...?* He certainly knew how to talk to people, - not! I told him that Mel was happily married and so he'd better forget any ideas he had in that direction. I then reminded him that we'd work to do and that I was his superior and that the conversation was closed.'

'Did you know that Mel met up with Mills at '*The Bull*'?'

'Yes. I told her she was crazy but she told me that she was only meeting up with him to put an end to him '*mothering*' her, once and for all.'

'Why did you think she was crazy to meet

him?'

'For one, I thought he was weird right from the first day at the library, and that given the circumstances, the way he'd been pestering her and everything well, I just thought it might send out the wrong signals.'

'You weren't just a little bit jealous, then? She'd turned you down for lunch but finds time to meet Derek'

'Me? No. And I don't like the way this is going now. I'll help you all I can because Mel was a friend of mine but I won't have things I say misconstrued.'

'Accept my apologies, Lynn.'

Lynn offered a terse, 'thank you.'

'So after the meeting at the pub with Mills, did Mel say any more about it?'

'She just said that she felt guilty about it. As if she was cheating on Geoff even though in her heart of hearts she knew the reason she'd gone and it wasn't to start an affair with Derek.'

'Did she mention how Derek behaved towards her after or during the meeting?'

'Only to say that he was already there when she arrived at the pub and that when she walked in he waved and beckoned to her. He was obviously pleased to see her. Pleased that she had turned up, I shouldn't wonder.'

'Anything more?'

'Not much. She just told me that when she went over and sat down he told her that he didn't really expect her to turn up. She said she told him that she shouldn't really be there and that as far as she was concerned he was just a work colleague. She told me the odd thing was that when she told him he just said '*and*?' She said she was amazed at that and said '*Derek, I have to go now', see you at work on Thursday'*. To which he replied, '*your loss'*.'

'Was there a cooling in the atmosphere between them at work?'

'I would say not on Mel's side. She just wanted to carry on being friendly. Pretending nothing had ever happened. With Derek though, it was different. He just cut her dead. Barely spoke to her all week. You could see it was getting to Mel, but what could she do? She didn't want to complain too much in case it gave Derek the wrong idea. She decided to just let the thing run its course.'

'Anything else you can add?'

'No. Not that I can think of at the moment.'

'Well, thanks Lynn. I'd better let you get back to work. Miss Jackson will think we've kidnapped you. We will have to talk to you again however. Will you be at home anytime tomorrow?'

'I finish here at three tomorrow, if that's any good?'

Craig drove back to the station. There was just so much information. Evans would go through it and no doubt tell Craig what he thought of it all. It seemed to Craig that Mel was just unfortunate to get mixed up with the man she had. Annie Gibbons he thought, had had a lucky escape.

'Will you be coming over to Lynn Davies' with me sir?' Craig asked.

'No. You can go alone. I can see from your notes that everything's pretty much under control. Just make sure you push a bit more, get every ounce you can from Lynn. She seems to be the only reliable source we've got, - apart from Annie Gibbons. Those photographs were a piece of evidence we desperately needed. They came through just in time.'

'I thought it was funny sir, how things suddenly came together like they did. I hope we're not missing something?'

'I doubt it Craig. Police work isn't all intrigue you know. Sometimes things just fall right. This is one of those times. You'll be off to see Geoff Ellis now then?'

'I was hoping to leave that until a little later.'

'No,' Evans countered, 'I should get along now. He'll be expecting you!'

Craig didn't get much from Geoff Ellis. He did however seem surprised to find out that Annie Gibbons had been interviewed. '*I bet she couldn't wait to tell you about Derek, could she*?'

'She only mentioned that Keith Davies was best man at your wedding.'

'That was a long time ago now, sergeant. All in the past. I'd prefer to keep it there if you don't mind.'

'I'm afraid we can't do that, Mr Ellis. Your past seems to be tying quite a tight knot around the present. If you think about it, I'm sure you'll understand.'

The following afternoon Craig called in to see Lynn Davies. He arrived just after four o'clock. She was at home alone. When questioned by Craig she said that her husband was working and wouldn't be home until after five. Craig acted puzzled.

'Was your husband a friend or acquaintance of Geoff's?'

'No. I met Mike while I was working on the late night checkout at Mather's food store. He came in one night just before closing, can you believe? When I tell you we closed at two in the morning, you'll understand why it was so funny. I'd seen him in the shop before but never spoken to him. Little did I know he was coming in the shop to see me. Had a bit of a crush on me, or so it seems! Anyway, something must've clicked as we married six months later.'

'Who married first, you or Mel?'

'Me. Mike and I had been married for about eight or nine months before Geoff came on the scene.'

'This job, I thought you'd gone straight from working in the theatre at Southport, to the library here, when did you find time to fit this evening job in?'

'I was saving up. Going off to see the world. I think going off to New Zealand with Mel had whetted my appetite, but as you can see, the way things turned out I didn't get very far! Ended up marrying Mike and settling in Newham.'

'Where did Mel meet Geoff, do you know?'

'I'm not really sure.'

'But you were living in a flat together.'

'Yes. But we weren't living in each other's pockets. She never brought him back to the flat, not as far as I know. I'm sorry I can't be of more help there.'

'She never mentioned that she'd met anyone, then?'

'Not to me. And if you think of it, I'd married Mike nearly twelve months before, so I'd been out of the flat for ages before Mel got married, and, when she did marry it was a pretty whirlwind affair. Me and Mike weren't even invited. I only ever met Geoff when he picked her up from the library.'

'Odd isn't it, not to be invited to your friend's wedding.'

'You can say or think whatever you like. I'm just telling you the way it happened.'

'Right. To get back to Derek Mills. You said that his attitude towards Mel had cooled. Can you tell me some more about their day to day relationship at work? It would probably be best if you think more recently now. Focus on the time before Mel disappeared.'

'Well, I'll start a little bit farther back if I might. Before Mel met Derek in the pub he'd been teasing her. I suppose in his way he was flirting with her. He'd come up behind her and make her jump. I could tell by her face that even though she was saying all the right things about being happily married and telling Derek he was just a '*work colleague*', that *part* of her actually liked the attention he was paying her. I still thought he was odd and told Mel to watch it but as I said, she didn't see the harm in anyone. She didn't confide in me though, so it was quite difficult to know what was really going on with Mel. I know she would talk general work things to him. When he hadn't been there long she took the trouble to have her break when he did and she was truly interested in how he was settling in at the library.'

'Didn't you think it was strange that she should arrange to have her breaks with him?'

'It wasn't that odd, not really. Mel was a department manager, she could take her breaks to suit herself.'

'Department manager in a library?'

'We all have our own stock rows to manage. The library manager is in over all charge but we have teams who are in charge of particular genres. Mel was in charge of foreign and English literature. All the poetry and classics, plus books written in their original language, such as Madame Bovary or Anna Karenina. If you wanted those books Mel was the person to see. She was a good stock manager. More or less could tell you every title that was on the shelves.'

'I see.'

'Is that all?'

'No, sorry,' Craig looked at his notes. 'Derek told me that you wanted Mel to go to '*The Bull*' for lunch, it was a Tuesday and he said that she told you she was tired and that she made other arrangements with you.'

'He said that? I didn't know he'd been around when we had that conversation.'

'Can you enlighten us further?'

'Yes. I had asked Mel to come to '*The Bull'* with me for lunch. It was a Tuesday and she always finished at one o'clock, so I thought it would be ok, but Mel made excuses. I told her that we hadn't been out much at all, not even for lunch since she became Mrs Ellis. I've mentioned this before, but it's true. Before she married Geoff it was one of our regular haunts, every Tuesday, lunch at '*The Bull'*. After she married I bet we were lucky if she managed to make lunch once every two or three months. I was married as well, but Mike didn't keep me under lock and key. I'd like to have seen him try! Anyway, like I said, we weren't the closest of friends but we were friends and I just couldn't accept the changes that had taken place, and all in under three years. I must've sounded a bit annoyed because she suddenly said, '*oh, all right Lynn, but it'll have to be next Tuesday, and I won't forget, I'll pencil it in'*. I was quite relieved and said '*great then, we'll do it'*.'

'You never got to keep the lunch date,' Craig said.

'No. Awful isn't it. You know, when I was a child I had the fancy that if I had plans made for the days ahead, something like a friend's party or a visit to Gran's, I felt that even though these things were perhaps only planned in 'my head', that I would be safe. Safe from the *'bad men'* that mum used to warn me about. As long as you had plans you would carry on, be untouchable. That was my philosophy as a child. It's a good job you don't know some things as a child, that you're allowed some 'fantasy', don't you think?'

'It's a good job that children can make up their own worlds where they're safe. That's what I think.'

'Sorry sergeant, I'm getting off the track. What else did you want to know?'

'Just tell me whatever you can about Mel; her behaviour in the days before she disappeared.'

'Nothing changed really. Derek was still giving her his cool act and at first it seemed odd to me that she had to get straight home to Geoff that Tuesday lunchtime but after Mel had left the library the thought just went from my head and I didn't think any more of it. When she came in the next day she was bright and bubbly and she was just '*Mel*', so I guess everything was all right. She actually said when I spoke to her later in the day that she couldn't wait to get home that night. I just said '*oh, a good night planned have you*?' and she said, '*not really, but we've been married twenty-eight months and six days, or in English money two years four months and six days, and I just want to get home*'. Don't quote me on the exact times here. I might be wrong, but that was one thing Mel never was. She knew how long she'd been married down to the exact day. Can you believe it? I asked her once how she remembered like that and she said, '*because I'm happy, I suppose*'.'

'Did Derek have a thing for Mel right from the start?'

'I should say so. The morning Miss Jackson asked us into the office to meet the new member of staff, I thought then, '*he fancies Mel*'. He just couldn't keep his eyes off her and then you should've seen his face when he was told he would be working with me in the morning. Chin almost dropped to his shoes. He soon perked up though when he found that in the afternoon he'd be working with Mel. He was just so obvious. That's why I don't understand how he could've turned so cold towards her. It was as if he'd just been switched off. It wasn't as if he was a human being at all, with feelings and emotions. He behaved like a robot, as if he was programmed. Do you know what I mean? I'm afraid I'm not making much sense.'

'You're doing fine, Lynn, don't worry, you're making perfect sense. You're giving us a picture to work with and that's just what we want.'

Lynn carried on, 'When we were back in the library I told Mel that I thought Derek fancied her. She just shrugged it off, but that first time I reckon she blushed a little, you know. It was almost as if really she quite enjoyed the fact that someone other than her husband had his eye on her. It was a bit like being back at school, I thought, when your hormones kick in and you realise *'boys exist'.'*

There was the sound of a key in the lock. Lynn's husband had returned. Craig got ready to leave. He passed Mike Davies in the hall.

'What did he want?' Mike asked as he came into the house, after watching Craig walk to his car.

'Just asking more questions about Mel and work and Derek. It's hard to remember sometimes everything that's gone on but I think I'm being accurate.'

'He seems to be spending a lot of time interviewing you,' Mike said. 'I thought you had a lot of staff at the library. Can't someone else help with the enquiries?'

'I suppose they would, and he has questioned everyone. But I knew Mel, remember? We shared a flat together. I'm someone who perhaps knows a little more about her.'

'No one could know what made Mel tick. She was a bit strange if you ask me.'

'No one's asking you, and Mel wasn't strange.'

'She was. If she'd have been your average girl, she would've made sure she married a man, not an excuse for one.'

'That's not a very nice thing to say.'

'It might not be, but it's the truth.'

Evans stayed in the office. What he'd thought had been a 'dead cert' theory, now seemed as unlikely as ever. Everyone they interviewed could be a possible suspect. He wasn't sure that any of them were telling the truth.

At home Angie Evans was drinking coffee with a neighbour. Christine and her husband Don had only moved into the area three months ago. They were still finding their feet. Angie had bumped into Christine at the supermarket and had invited her to '*come round for coffee*'.

'Your husband's in the police?'

A little taken aback by Christine's sudden dive into conversation, Angie mumbled, 'yes. Yes he is.'

'Is he looking into what happened to Mel from the library?'

'I can't say. He never discusses his work with me.'

'I don't believe that. He must tell you something!'

Angie wasn't keen on Christine's forthright attitude and wished she'd not bumped into her at all. She wasn't in the mood for this kind of conversation. 'No, he doesn't,' she replied truthfully, 'he never mentions work to me at all.'

'Oh, I couldn't do with that. I question Don about what he's been up to all the time. I want to know everything. I wouldn't like it if he didn't tell me everything right down to the last detail. It would drive me mad.'

Angie thought, *You're driving me mad*, but then asked, 'What does your husband do, for work?'

'He works for James and Jenks, the hauliers in town. He's a driver.'

Angie asked, 'Does he work away from home or is it all local stuff?'

'He's away three nights a week, Monday, Tuesday, Wednesday. I see him on Thursday evening after he finishes and then he's home, working on Friday. Most weekends he's off, so that's nice. What about yours?'

'Stuart's always worked odd hours. He tends to 'phone if he's going to be very late but it's not a nine till five job. I've just had to get used to it.'

Christine smiled at her new friend. Angie was just wishing she hadn't invited her. She found her too brash and wished the whole event was over. Nevertheless she found herself offering Christine more coffee.

Evans sat formulating more theories in his head. What did he know about any of them? He got himself a cup of coffee from the machine and sat at his desk picking the meat from the bones. What had he learned? He was actually quite glad when Craig returned. He could bounce some of his theories off him, see what he thought.

'Geoff was a quiet sort of bloke to all intents and purposes. Even though he was a writer, he always kept his two lives separate, one from the other. In one he was the brash journalist who happened to have film star good looks, but with Mel he was different. He was quiet and attentive. And in a way that made him suitable material for Mel. Until Geoff came along, no-one had really given Mel much attention. She was always the little mouse cowering in the background. She let her '*friends*' take the attention and she was glad they did. Her friends weren't close, ever. There was not a person she knew that she would ever, truly give away any secrets too. She kept her hand close to her heart. Mel put barriers up around her, and even her closest friend Lynn, had never been able to really get to know Mel that much. She was an enigma and yet, those who met her seemed to get along fine with her. To everyone she was the perfect person. She was somebody you would be pleased to call your '*friend*', so', said D I Evans after going through Craig's notes and his own thoughts, '*we've not a great deal more to go on.*'

Evans had a hunch that Miss Jackson knew

more than she was letting on. He thought he'd go and see her and see where it got him.

Miss Jackson was just how you'd imagine a librarian to be, if you'd been brought up in the 40's. She had silver grey hair cut very short. He seemed to remember an aunt of his had her hair in this style years ago. It was called, if he remembered correctly, a 'semi shingle'. The thought made him smile. She wore a tweed two piece, a skirt and jacket and to complete the picture, sensible brown brogues and wire rimmed glasses. She gave out a sense of old fashioned authority, '*old fashioned*' being the operative words.

Evans had been shown into the library office where she was waiting for him. She was looking at her computer screen and busy '*clicking*' away. She had some county business that just 'had to be finished' she said. She would be with him shortly. Evans thought that in another life she might be prison officer material. She seemed cut out for it and she was definitely using all the tactics. Making him wait, being one.

After a few more minutes, Miss Jackson looked up and over her glasses across the desk at Evans,

'Well now, that's finished, what can I help you with Inspector?'

'I just need to ask a few more questions about Melanie.'

'Yes?'

'I'm intrigued about Geoff and Mr Mills, Mr Mills who was employed here at the library. Were he and Geoff friendly, towards each other?'

'Friendly enough, I suppose. I didn't really see

that much of them together, unless Geoff stepped inside sometimes while he was waiting for Melanie to finish.'

'Did he do that often?'

'Meet her from work, do you mean?'

'Yes.'

'All the time, if she was working late. Not that we were that late you understand, but particularly in the winter once the clocks had changed, he'd always collect her. He remarked once that he didn't like her coming past the common on her own. He always seemed very protective of her.'

'So the night she disappeared, that was unusual that he didn't meet her then. It was unusual that she should end up walking home with Derek Mills?'

'I suppose it was. I'd just never thought about it before.'

'When you say you don't work late, I notice from your opening hours that you're open three nights in the week until eight- thirty Do you ever work later than this?'

'Only when there're special open evenings. We only do them, what, a maximum of six evenings a year. And by that I mean the exhibition by the local arts group or an occasional lecture. That type of thing.'

'Was there anything like that the night Mel went missing?'

'I don't think so. I could check.'

'If you wouldn't mind.'

Miss Jackson clicked on to her computer. She brought calendars and charts down and looked through them. Evans was watching her all the while she did this.

'I'm sorry. There was nothing that night. It was a usual eight-thirty finish.'

'So normally Geoff would have met her then?'

'Yes, I suppose he would have done.'

'Did you see him anywhere? Did he come into the library?'

'I was working late that night to get end of month figures ready to send off to county. I'm afraid I would be up in this office. I wouldn't see what was going on downstairs in the library.'

'How do the staff leave the premises? Is there a staff exit?'

'There is. Once the library is locked at the front and we've made sure that there is no-one else left in the building, the lights are dimmed and we leave via the rear of the building. If we are all leaving together I always make sure the building is locked, Mr Graham the caretaker is in the building with me until I'm ready to go. It's a security measure.'

'And if you're on your own, as you were the night Mel disappeared?'

'I'm never altogether on my own. Mr Graham is here. He cannot finish until I am ready to leave.'

'Do you work late often, Miss Jackson?'

'I try not to. It's only really when the monthly figures have to go through to county that I'm late, and then it's no more than twenty minutes. I do try and get everything done in the working day. It is the exception rather than the rule, Inspector.'

Miss Jackson smiled as she spoke and emphasis was definitely on the '*Inspector*'.

She's had enough of me, Evans thought.

'I won't take up any more of your time Miss Jackson. You've been most helpful. Thank you.'

Craig wasn't back when Evans arrived at the office. He had gone to interview Mills' mother again. The thought ran through his head, *why did someone who was as likeable as Mel end up with such strange people around her. Even her boss, Miss Jackson, seemed odd.*

Craig breezed into the office about two hours later.

'Did she have a lot to tell you, Mrs Mills?' Evans asked.

'Quite a lot. She seemed happier to talk this time. It's all very interesting. Interesting and strange.'

'Everything about this case is strange. Try and surprise me, go on.'

'Mrs Mills says that Derek had a girlfriend at the library and she was called Mel.'

'Funny, it didn't ring any bells last time.'

'Well it didn't, but she's spoken now, and Derek isn't her son as such. He was adopted. He was a baby, only months old when Mrs and the late Mr Mills took him into their home and she says from very early on she regretted it. He wasn't a particularly nice child. Mr Mills told her she took things too much to heart and it was only '*boys being boys*' but she said she was glad when he left home. It gave her some peace of mind.'

'Everything was like a fairy tale the last time you spoke to her. She's changed her tune, quite a lot, actually.'

'Now this is the really interesting thing. Derek went to New Zealand, she said, I have checked it out and he did actually spend two years working on a farm and guess where that was?'

'Waikiri, where Mel came from?'

'Exactly.'

'So, they knew one another before?'

'May have done. It's probably a long shot, but what a coincidence.'

'From what his mum said, his dad went over there twice to visit.'

'Pity he's not here to ask.'

'He died two years ago.'

'What about the girlfriend from the library. What about Mel?'

'Well, I've got a photo' of her. I think you'll recognise her.'

Craig handed the photo' across to Evans.

'It's Lynn!', he said, 'this whole business just becomes more absurd by the minute. I'm beginning to feel as though I'm on a merry go round.'

Derek Mills was re- interviewed. They showed him the photo' they had of Lynn.

'It came from your mother,' Craig said, 'how do you explain that?'

'I don't think I can. Have you spoken to Lynn?'

'Are you worried about what she's told us? Don't be. Just tell us the truth, give us some explanations. Mel's dead, you profess to have been in love with her, give us the truth.'

'That photo', it was taken on a day out. We

organised a trip to 'Monkey Land'. It wasn't all apes. They had a 'rope walk' area. You could climb and be above the enclosures and see everything with a bird's eye view. It was fantastic. The photo' was taken there. It was last summer.'

'I take it this was a trip taken by most of the library staff?'

'Yes, we all went, Lynn and her husband, Mike and Mel and Geoff. We even got Miss Jackson and Mr Graham to attend, but they stayed in the zoo area. We all met up later and went for a meal in the restaurant, at the park. I think we all had a really good time.'

'Did anyone else come, with Miss Jackson and Mr Graham?'

'Miss Jackson came on her own. Mr Graham's wife came with him.'

'How did you end up telling your mother you had a girlfriend at the library and showing her the photo' with you and Lynn on it?'

'Mum was dying for me to settle down, get hitched. When I left home I think she thought I would be moving in with somebody, a girl. It never happened. When the photos came back I thought it would keep her quiet for a while if I told her I had a girlfriend. I just said it was Lynn because she was next to me on the photograph.'

'Why did you say she was called Mel? You could have easily kept the names correct.'

'Mel was the one I happened to be in love with.'

'And your mother believed you?'

'I think so. She never asked to meet her. I

suppose she could've done at some time. Anyway she didn't, so it didn't really matter. It was easier for me when dad was alive. I think he understood me. I often wondered about that, wondered whether dad was '*all he cracked on to be*'. He was always a man's man, you see. I think now there may have been a different dad hidden away under the surface. I wonder whether dad was more like me than could possibly be expected. Maybe there was more of a need for his '*men friends*' than we'll ever really know. I'm adopted. Still, I suppose mum couldn't wait to tell you that. She told everyone almost as soon as they'd brought me home; as if to wash her hands of any responsibility she had for me, to show that there was no way I could ever be her son. I was never good enough, you see. Sorry, what was the question?'

'You're covering more than enough ground Mr Mills, but I was just wondering, did your mother never once drop hints about wanting to meet your girlfriend?'

'No. I don't know why, she was pretty keen on most people I knew, on meeting them. Perhaps it was something that she would've got round to.'

'Did Lynn or Mel know about this deception?'

'No.'

'The night Mel disappeared, you've acknowledged that you drugged her. Is that all that happened that evening?'

'I've told you. I didn't do it. You need to speak to Geoff Ellis.'

'Geoff Ellis. Is he your lover?'

'No. That was all over a long time ago.'

'But you came here to get a job at the library. Are you sure you didn't know Geoff was in Newham? It would have been easy to find out he was living here with his wife. You knew she worked at the library. You knew you could get close to him, carry on where you'd left off. You wanted to renew your relationship with Geoff, didn't you? That was the only reason that you came here. You got to him through his wife Melanie. You couldn't let him have a chance at a life with the woman he loved. You loved him and you wanted to get him back and if that meant that Mel had to be got rid of, then you'd do it, wouldn't you?'

'No, no, no. I've told you. I didn't do it.'

Derek had his head in his hands as the tone of Craig's voice rose still higher.

'You know what, I don't think you know what's true and what isn't any more, and because of that, Mel Ellis is dead. We know you went over to New Zealand for a while. Is that where you first met Mel?'

'I don't know what you're talking about.'

'But you have been in New Zealand, haven't you.'

'Yes. But that was a long time ago now. I was out there working. I was there for about two years.'

'You're saying you didn't know Mel, then?'

'That's what I'm saying. I didn't know her.'

Angie Evans knew that Stuart was fumbling through this case. Her words, not his.

He just knew that everything about the case

was odd, including most of the suspects. He would get Craig to interview Lynn again tomorrow. He would go and have a '*cosy chat*' with Mr Ellis, see if he couldn't break him down, in a purely professional way of course.

Angie chatted away to Stuart, hoping she wasn't getting on his nerves. She knew it was a fine line and she didn't want to cross it.

'Had Christine, our new neighbour round for coffee today. Don't think I shall bother again. She's not my type of person, very brash.'

'And you're not?' Stuart replied.

He was slumped in an armchair, staring at a blank TV screen. Angie Evans came through and joined him.

'I may be a lot of things Stuart, but this Christine woman takes the biscuit. If I ever try to be '*friendly*' to people I don't really know, just drag me back inside will you? I'm hoping she doesn't return the call. I don't think I could sit through another two hours of mindless conversation, because that's all it was. We've nothing in common. Nothing at all, well, perhaps maybe our husbands. You seem to both work strange hours.'

'What does 'Mr Christine' do then, that keeps him out of the house?'

'He's a lorry driver.'

Angie sat down next to Stuart. She picked up the remote and brought the t v to life.

'If we're sitting here', she said, 'we may as well have something to look at.'

The evening passed in silence. Angie was used

to this. She knew that Stuart wouldn't make conversation, even with her, when his mind was on other things. It was on other things now. She knew he was thinking about the Mel Ellis case. She knew better than to break his conversational silence with bits of nothing. Her talk of small town conflicts would be irrelevant. She looked at him. He didn't seem to notice, even though he was next to her. It was only ten o'clock, she placed the remote on the coffee table in front of them,

'I'm going to bed, now,' she said, and left Stuart alone with his thoughts. He didn't reply. He didn't even seem to notice that she was going.

The next morning, Craig was already at his desk when Evans arrived.

'You look rough, sir.'

'Thanks, I've been up most of the night trying to make all the pieces fit. They don't.'

'You want me to go and interview Lynn again this morning?'

'Yes. I'll come with you. We can go from there to see Geoff Ellis. I've decided I'll tag along. I thought yesterday that I might see Ellis alone, but I think we might just bring him down to the station with us later. That might do the trick. I'm still sure that he's the key to all this. When have you arranged to go and see Lynn?'

'Nine-thirty this morning. She's off today. Struggling with a cold but she said that we could still go round.'

'I'll have a coffee and then we'll go. It might

loosen her tongue if she's kept waiting for another half hour.'

When they arrived at Lynn's they could see that she had just been on the 'phone to someone. They had seen her through the frosted glass of her front door. She couldn't hide. She was on full view.

'Good of you to see us, Lynn,' Evans said, 'and at such short notice. Are you feeling well enough to talk, we could come back later?'

'I'll be fine, thank you. I was just 'phoning the surgery, see if I could get an appointment this evening. They're fully booked.'

She's a smart one, already covering her tracks and we've not even started to question her yet. Evans thought.

'No, you find that,' Evans replied, 'they never seem to be able to fit you in. I think the receptionists sometimes act as a first line of defence. You've got to know how to work them.'

Lynn showed them into the lounge,

'Please, sit down.'

'I know you must think that we're always asking questions. It seems like that to us as well, but we're breaking through. We're almost there and any more help you could give would be appreciated,' Craig began, 'now we've a photograph we'd like you to have a look at. You're on it, as is Derek Mills. Can you tell us about the photograph?'

'Yes, as much as there is to know. It was taken last summer at 'Monkey World, we'd gone on a trip from the library. We had a great day.'

'Did Mel and Geoff Ellis go?'

'Yes, we all went I think, even Mr Graham, the

caretaker, he came along and brought his wife.'

'Was there any argument between Geoff and Mel?'

'Were they rowing, do you mean?'

'Yes.'

'No. I've never seen Mel argue or disagree with anyone. If they did when they were at home, well, I don't know, but on that day, no, they didn't have an argument.'

'What about Derek, did he get on with everyone, particularly Mel and Geoff, any disputes there that you were aware of?'

'None. It was a fantastic day. Everyone enjoyed it.'

'Who organised it?'

'No one in particular. It wasn't like we had to book or anything. Derek brought the info' in and kind of suggested it would be good to go as a group. We sorted dates and went, that's all there was to it.'

'I know we've been over this before, but in the weeks before Mel's death, how did Derek behave toward her?'

'I've really told you all I know about that. He was always the same. It was obvious from the start that he had a crush on her.'

'Did she like the attention?'

'I think she did. I've told you, we weren't that close even though we shared a flat together but I'd never seen anyone pay any attention to her, and then she met Geoff and it was pretty much full steam ahead. So, although I don't believe she would ever have cheated on Geoff I think she found Derek's attentions ...flattering.'

'She milked it a bit, is that what you're saying?'

'I think she did to a degree. Yes.'

'Were you jealous of the attention that Derek gave her?'

'I think we've been down this avenue before. I don't know what you want me to admit to or say, but no, I wasn't jealous.'

'What about Geoff, how did he feel about all this, do you know?'

'I don't know. I suppose if it had been me, leading on someone, knowing there was nothing going to come of it, well my husband would've been down on me like a ton of bricks. That's one thing I will say, Geoff was really quite quiet. He behaved like a gentleman. He was always like that. I suppose that's why he would meet Mel if we had to work late. He looked after her.'

'Interesting phrase you used there, Lynn, '*leading someone on*'. Do you think Mel was leading Derek on?'

'Not intentionally, no. But then that was Mel. She probably didn't realise that every little word or gesture that she used when she befriended people could have been misconstrued by Derek. He probably thought that he was in with a chance. Everyone else could see it was hopeless, but not Derek. In some ways he was a bit of a lap dog, happy to pick up any crumbs that were left.'

'Did you go to their wedding?'

'No. I've already told you that. They married pretty quick. It was a quiet affair. Mel wanted a church wedding so that's what they had, but there were no relatives there, and only a handful of friends. Of course Mel's family were all in New Zealand and Geoff didn't have any close family so, it was very quiet. I don't even think there was a reception, as such. I think a few of them went to the '*White Lion*' for a meal afterwards. As I've said, it wasn't a big affair. But Mel could be like that, she never liked a lot of fuss, but one thing I do know is that she did love Geoff.'

'Are you sure, I mean after what you've just said it seems that their relationship might not have been as strong as you might have thought.'

'It was strong all right. I just think Mel could be a little bit soft sometimes.'

'We know that Geoff always met Mel if she was working late at the library, why didn't he meet her the night of her disappearance?'

'I'm afraid I don't know. He wasn't outside when we left. I drove home. I even offered Mel a lift but she said she would walk, that she would probably meet up with Geoff on the way home.'

'Did you see Derek anywhere near the library that evening?'

'He came across the car park as I was walking to my car. I waved to him and said that I would see him in the morning. He said that he didn't know for definite that he would be in. He'd had to come back to check with Miss Jackson. She was supposed to have 'phoned him, but the call had never materialised. He said the work sheets had been filled in wrong or something and she'd got too many staff in. He wasn't bothered because he was taking his car in for its MOT. Then he said that he was hoping to sell it. I think he was mad. It was a lovely car. I wouldn't have wanted to get rid of it, not for anything, but he said that it drank up too much petrol, that he couldn't afford to keep it on the road.'

'What car was this?'

'It was quite old, a green E Type, he called it. I thought it was lovely. He drove to work in it sometimes, not often but...' Lynn began to cough. I think I'll just get a drink if you don't mind, would you like one?'

Lynn returned from the kitchen with three cups of coffee. Evans added three spoons of sugar to the mix.

'Doesn't your wife tell you that too much sugar is a bad thing?' Lynn joked.

'She tells me a lot of things,' Evans replied, his face as steely as it was when he entered the room.

Evans asked a question now, taking over the reins from Craig. Craig knew he sometimes played it like this so he was used to it.

'Would I be correct in thinking that Mr Mills was a joker?'

'Yes. He got on most everyone's nerves at times. In the library, he'd either tell schoolboy type jokes that were really so banal a six year old wouldn't laugh, or he'd just keep saying silly things to irritate you. He was a master of his art.'

'Did he irritate you?'

'Sometimes. I think he irritated Mel more than me.'

'Why do you say that?'

'They did for a time have a joke amnesty. Mel

allowed him three jokes a day, any more than that and he was sent to Coventry, in the nicest possible way of course. It was against Mel's nature to be unkind.'

'Who were you speaking to on the 'phone when we arrived?'

'I haven't spoken to anyone.'

'You were on the 'phone when we arrived, you said it was the doctor's surgery.'

'Oh that. Yes, I was trying to get an evening appointment but it was impossible.'

'I see.'

Evans turned and walked across to the window. He wasn't sure, but he thought he could see Geoff Ellis at the end of the street. He took a drink of his coffee.

'Your husband, Lynn, where does he work?'

'I thought I'd already told you that, weeks ago. He's at Hammond's in town. He's a mechanic, but he's not always based here. A lot of the time he's away. Most of his week is spent in Worcester.'

'That's odd for a mechanic, isn't it?'

'Our whole life is odd, believe me. We'd only been married a few months when he was offered a promotion. That meant leaving here and moving to Worcester. We actually looked at houses but I wasn't really certain about the idea. Mike loved it though. He'd have moved right away, I wasn't so sure. It might end up that we do move though. I'm finding the weeks pretty lonely without him. Not that I'd say as much to him. He needs the job, daren't give it up on a whim, eh!'

'Do you love your husband Mrs Davies?'

'I think you should retract that last question. I allowed you into my home and ... what is all this any way? Surely I'm not a suspect now? I've helped you all I can and ...I was a friend of Mel's. I could never hurt her.' Lynn sat down and started to cry. 'I don't think I want to answer any further questions. I'd like you to leave.'

Evans turned to face Lynn, 'that's all right Mrs Davies. I'm sorry to upset you. That wasn't the intention. We'll be off now and it is possible that you won't be seeing any more of us, but should we need to talk to you I hope you'll make yourself available.'

'I suppose so. It's just that last remark, it wasn't called for.'

Evans and Craig left, Craig said, 'you certainly ruffled her feathers, sir, what was all that about?'

'Geoff Ellis was at the end of the street. He's not home and dry yet. And why was he there? Pound to a penny it was Geoff she was on the 'phone to when we arrived. She's no more a cold than I'm Prime Minister.'

'She's not being entirely truthful, then?'

'Far from it, I'd say. I think they're both in it up to their eye balls, but I don't know why, and I don't know why Derek Mills is involved either.'

'Changed your mind about him then? I thought from the start you were sure it was him.'

'I was. I'm not so certain now. I just find it odd that you'd share a flat with someone, go off and visit their parents with them; particularly when these parents happen to live in New Zealand, then both get jobs at the same library, and then you don't know about, and are not invited to this '*friend's*' wedding. Lynn also mentioned that the lunches at '*The Bull'* had all but dried up. She more or less had to force Mel to go. I think they'd fallen out. Mel didn't like arguments or bad feeling, so it was probably easier for her just to try and 'avoid' Lynn. We'll see, but it's just a hunch. What we do need to do is go and have a look at Derek's '*green car'*. That's a bit of information we didn't have before, so back to the station and another word with Derek if you wouldn't mind Craig, then it's off to see the grieving husband.'

When they arrived back the duty clerk had a message for them from Mrs Bruce, the desk sergeant informed them that, '*she wants to know when the body will be released for burial. She wants to get on with things.'*

'I don't think it'll be much longer now,' Evans said, 'we're almost there.'

'Shall I tell her that?'

'Yes. If she's asking about dates, I can't say but let her book things as much as she can. Tell her I'll be in touch personally within the week.'

Craig looked up, 'you're feeling optimistic now?'

'You know Craig, I think I am.'

Craig was sent off to interview Derek. Mills was surprised to see him.

'We need to clarify one or two points with you,' Craig said.

Mills began talking as though he were at his

home, not a small holding cell with a constable standing sentry.

'Sit down', Mills offered, 'what is it I can help you with?'

'We have reason to believe you own a car. A green E. type.'

'Where is the car Mr Mills?'

'I don't have a car, sergeant.'

'Are you sure? We can check you know.'

Mills had been standing; he now turned and sat down.

'I'm not lying. I never have owned a car.'

'You've been seen driving one, to your place of work. You parked a green E. type at the library.'

Mills laughed, 'That old thing?'

'I suppose. Can you tell me a little more about the car Mr Mills? People believed it was yours.'

'I don't know why they should think it was mine. I perhaps exaggerated a little. It was a bit flash I suppose. It's not mine. It belongs to Geoff Ellis.'

'Why would he let you drive his car? What was the point?'

'It was a sort of code.'

'What sort of code?'

'He used it as a code for, for ...Lynn.'

'Lynn Davies?'

'Yes. They were having an affair. It meant he would be able to meet her later that evening. Her husband's a mechanic you see, but you must know that. Geoff would go round to her house when Mike was away, but he liked to let Lynn know he was free. Mel belonged to a reading group and a yoga club. Mel knew he went out on the evenings she wasn't home. He told her he went to the pub for an hour.'

'Did Mel know about the car?'

'She probably thought it was mine. I gave her a lift home in it sometimes.' He laughed. 'It's all rather strange and tangled this whole thing, isn't it?'

Craig had to admit it was. *Poor Mel*! Nothing in her short life had been straightforward. She was being deceived at every angle.

'Didn't Mel question his 'nights out'?'

'Geoff was always good at covering his tracks. I told you, he said he went down the pub. He has had plenty of practice, sergeant, his whole life is one built on deceit. Mills smiled. Craig's hate for this person was deep. He wondered if Mills had any idea.

'Where is the car now?'

'It's at Took's on Melbourne Street. It didn't pass its MOT. It's due to be picked up tomorrow. I think Geoff will be selling it on as soon as he can.'

'Thanks. Why does it take so long to get an answer from you?'

'I think that is more than obvious. I'm not going anywhere. I'll still be here.'

Evans found the whole scenario compelling. Evans wanted to talk to Lynn again. This time he wouldn't be so courteous. It wasn't doing him any favours being a gentleman. He wanted Lynn to spill the beans. He thought he knew what had happened now and how they all were involved in it but he wanted Lynn to confirm it. From what Craig had told him, Mills would soon come clean too. He was evidently finding the whole thing a strain. Ellis? Ellis could wait a while, Evans had plans for him, but he wouldn't be rushed.

As soon as Craig left, Mills started to rant at the constable. Said he wanted to see a priest, said he had to tell someone about what had happened the night Mel disappeared. The constable sensed the urgency in his voice, and got Craig to return. Once Craig was back in the cell with him, Mills became tight-lipped. It seems he didn't want to talk at all, and he'd lost the need for a priest.

Craig left and he and Evans went round again to the home of Lynn Davies

'Oh, hello, I didn't expect to see you back here so soon.'

'I'm sure you didn't' Craig replied, 'but you knew we'd be back, didn't you. That's why you dropped the hint about the car, isn't it? You wanted us to come back. You need to tell us more.'

'You'd better come in.'

Craig and Evans entered the room that they'd had left only an hour or two before.

'Sit down,' she said, 'you may as well be comfortable.'

'Cold any better?' Evans asked.

'A little,' she replied.

'Good', Evans responded.

'What did you want to ask me?'

'Your affair with Geoff Ellis, how long has it been going on?'

'Just about forever.'

'We need more than that, Lynn.'

'I fell in love with Geoff when we were both at the paper in Malverton. I'd started as a junior reporter. He was a few years older than me and he was married then to Annie. We'd met just a few weeks after his marriage to Annie. It's awful the way things turn out, isn't it? Fate can be so cruel. But, with us it was the real thing. To try and get over him I moved away and moved back in with Mel. She still had the flat in Newham. A little later I took the job in the library. I didn't know Geoff's marriage had been annulled, and I genuinely don't know where he met Mel. I'd no idea that he would be anywhere near Newham and me. Time moved on and I decided to do my 'world trip'. I started working in the evenings at Mather's late night store. Well, then I met Mike. We had a whirlwind romance and married. It isn't a good marriage, Mike works away a lot. Anyway, after me and Mike married, I called round to the flat in Newham one night to collect some more of my things. I just couldn't believe it when Geoff opened the door. We just carried on where we'd left off.'

'Did your husband know about this relationship?'

'I don't think Mike bothered about anything I did. He was away so often, it was like we lived separate lives. And he'd always thought Geoff - he'd always believed Geoff preferred men. He knew about Geoff's younger days. I'd mentioned Derek to him. And I always assumed that Mike had affairs with other women. The morals of everything just didn't seem to matter. Here, our home, it was just a place to sleep and eat- a base.'

'And the car, whose idea was that?' Craig asked.

'Geoff's. He liked things to be done with an air of intrigue. I don't think he ever really grew up.'

'And Mel never knew about the two of you?'

'She suspected, but she was never really sure. I think that's why Mike and I weren't invited to the wedding. But recently she'd become suspicious again. She was cottoning on.'

'When do you think she became certain that there was something between you and Geoff?' Evans asked.

'Just a few weeks before she died.'

'And you stayed her friend?'

'No. She wouldn't have anything to do with me. After all I was the woman who had wrecked her life. That's where Derek came in.'

'He was the go between?' Craig asked.

'You could say that. You see he and Geoff had been lovers, a long time ago. It was all over and done with and Geoff was happy with me. But Mel got in the way. Geoff said it would be easy to get rid of her and I believed him. He said she wouldn't dream of a divorce. I don't know why, it's no big deal. We thought that after everything was done I would divorce Mike and then after a decent interval we would be able to marry.'

'Why not divorce Mel?'

'She wouldn't hear of it. He told me she was obsessive. She wasn't the timid person everyone thought her, me included. She could be quite aggressive when she wanted. He told me this was the only way. I believed him.'

'And Derek?' Craig continued.

'We knew he was still in love with Geoff. That's why he took the job at the library. He knew Geoff lived in the area. It was just pure coincidence that Mel happened to work there. Suddenly everything fell into place and to be honest, we couldn't believe our luck.'

The conversation came to an abrupt halt when the 'phone began to ring.

'Aren't you going to answer it?' Evans asked.

'I don't think it will be important. It can wait.'

'Craig, go and answer the 'phone will you?'

Evans noted the change in the demeanour of Lynn. She started to cry. Craig returned to the room.

'It was Ellis, for you Lynn. I expect he wanted to talk to you before we did. But as he found out, he's been too late.'

'Is he all right?'

'He'll be fine. There's a police presence outside his house. He can't go anywhere. And now, if you don't mind we'd like you to come with us, Lynn. If you'd like to get yourself ready.'

'Just give me a few moments.'

They arrived at the police station just after Ellis had been brought in.

'Has he admitted anything yet? 'Evans asked.

'Nothing,' came the reply.

'There's just one thing left for us to do now, Craig, that's go and have another chat with Derek

Mills.'

'Do you think he'll co operate?' Craig asked.

'Bound to,' Evans replied, 'in any case we've nearly got the whole of it from Lynn.'

Mills was ready for them when they returned.

'I knew you'd be back. I knew it couldn't go on much longer. It's just a pity about Mel, that's all. I did love her a little, you know.'

'Yes. But you loved Geoff more and that's where he had you, isn't it? You were prepared to do anything for him.'

'I was prepared to do too much for him, but I didn't kill her. He did it.'

'Would you like to elaborate for us Derek?' Craig asked.

'I may as well, we've come this far. What do you want to know?'

'Ellis killed his wife, we know that much, what part did you play in her death.'

'I just drugged her. We were standing outside the library, talking, joking. I knew Mel would be there until eight-thirty, when the library closed. I thought I'd best get there by eight o'clock. I had the pretence that I had to check my next day's hours with Miss Jackson. It was easy. Mel didn't really like my jokes, you know. We had an '*amnesty*' as she liked to call it. But I still teased her. She was really too nice a person to be mad at anybody, and if she was, it wasn't for long. She was lovely, you know. It's all so awful. And, I know I could've stopped it, I just wasn't strong enough.' Mills stopped, head in hands and began to cry.

Evans wanted to ask him *what the hell he was playing at,* to say, *why didn't you cry for the girl you helped murder, but he bit his tongue*. He wanted to hear the rest of the story from Mills.

'Carry on Derek,' Craig said.

He had seen Evans' face and knew he was staying quiet because he had to. He knew his boss and he knew that he had a short fuse. He didn't want it to blow here, not now.

Mills continued, 'We were outside the library, then we started talking about work rotas, very boring stuff. It was unusual for Geoff not to be there, waiting for her. Mel looked round for him. I knew where he was, where he was waiting. I knew what would come next. Mel said, '*I guess I'd better set off, I'll probably meet Geoff on the way, see you tomorrow.*' I looked at her and said, 'I think it might be the end of the road Mel.' She turned round to look at me and replied, '*wish you'd stop talking in riddles Derek.*' She was smiling and then she set off again, walking. I stood for a few seconds. I know I could've protected her, stopped what was going to happen but I realise now that I loved Geoff too much, and I'd promised him, *what could I do?* It seems so easy now to say I would've done the right thing. I know I'm as guilty as Geoff, and possibly Lynn. We were all her friends, you see, but we all turned on her, she hadn't a chance I suppose, from the day she married Geoff. Anyway, instead of protecting her I ran to catch up with her. I had the syringe in my pocket. I caught up with her and grabbed her arm, spun her round to me. I'll walk with you until we meet up with Geoff. I'll never forgive myself if I let you walk home alone. And do you know what she said to me? She said, '*you really are a big softy Derek. I'll forgive you the awful jokes. I'm glad of your company, come on.*' She just didn't know where it would end up. I just wish I could change it now, but I can't, it's too late.' Mills stopped again then said, 'just give me a while, I need a drink.'

He sipped water from a plastic cup that was on the table in front of him. After a couple of minutes he continued, 'We walked on to the spot on the common road where I knew Geoff had left the car. He wasn't in it, of course, he was at Lynn's, waiting. Mel spotted the car and said, '*what's your car doing here, Derek?*' I bluffed my way out of it and made a joke.

'Please Derek, joke amnesty, remember?'

'Then I looked at her and said the joke's on you, Mel. I took her hand and spun her towards me once more. I had the syringe in my hand. I used all the force I could muster with my right arm and plunged the syringe into her side. She just looked at me and said, *'what was that?'* I acted dumb. I said 'what?' Then she said that she felt sick, that she'd have to sit down. I walked her to the car and bundled her in. The rest was easy. I'd done the hard part. I drove home and 'phoned Geoff on his mobile. He was at Lynn's, her husband was away. I waited in the car with Mel beside me. If anyone passed by I put my arm round her, made it look like we were a couple. When Geoff arrived I got out of the car, gave him the keys and he drove off with Mel. He did the rest. That was it. My part was over.

All I can say is that I never wanted to hurt her. I'm sorry.'

'Why did you tell us in your first statement that you'd drugged her and kept her at your home? Why did you lie Derek?' Evans questioned.

'I was right in it. I knew that. You see, I was still in love with Geoff. I'd do anything to prove that to him. I thought that if I went along with the plan he'd realise that. Realise, perhaps that he still loved me. I thought he'd come back to me, leave Lynn. I believed that he couldn't really love her. He'd blundered with Mel hadn't he? So even though it was a long shot, it was one that I was prepared to take. I didn't believe that he would actually go through with it. I thought right up to the last that Mel would be safe. I thought I knew Geoff, you see. I didn't believe he was capable of murder.'

'But you helped him,' Craig said, 'Some might've said the same of you, that you couldn't hurt anyone, but you hurt Mel. You helped in her murder!'

'I know. I suppose it all seems so very odd, but anyway there's nothing more to add. Not here. Not at the moment. What will happen to Geoff and Lynn?'

'I wouldn't concern yourself with that, not now,' Evans replied. 'I'd just think about getting yourself a good lawyer.'

6 ONE GOOD TURN DESERVES…

Debbie was giddy with anticipation. She had cooked one of his favourite meals, chilli, nicely spicy. He wouldn't detect that added ingredient, of course he wouldn't.

When Paul arrived home, she'd show him how glamorous she could look. This marriage had cost her dear. Never mind, she would soon be promenading with someone new!

Paul entered the room, his jaw dropped,

'You're beautiful.'

'You've remembered!' she replied.

'I'll pour us a drink.' Paul said, thinking all the while how great Debbie looked. Why had he forgotten? He knew the answer to that, Tracy.

He heard Debbie's reply, 'Got one, from the chiller.'

Paul stared in disbelief, 'No!' he cried.

Within minutes Debbie's head was swimming, her mouth foaming. She fell to the floor.

'What is it'? she mumbled.

'Poison', Paul answered, 'Sorry.'

Leaving her there on the floor, Paul went to eat. He helped himself to a generous serving of chilli. He felt strange. He slumped forward, his head falling into the plate of chilli. He didn't say anything, wouldn't remember anything, couldn't do anything again, ever.

Debbie appeared in the doorway. She looked at the slumped body of her husband.

'Touché', she said and smiled.

7 DOLLS

As a child, Emma had little time for dolls; dolls with faces and features painted on to mimic a child's, looked to Emma to be exactly what they were not, dead babies. There was one exception to this, 'Rag Doll'. Emma cared for this doll, looked after it, and in the way of a child, babied it. Rag Doll, you see, had no pretence.

Emma was five or six years old when she conducted her first burial. She put her least favourite doll into a shoe box. The doll was dressed in its best clothes for the occasion, placed in the box and the lid taped down. These dolls didn't have names, but this didn't bother the child. She just wanted rid of them.

Some of the missing dolls had been gifts for the 'favourite girl', the 'little princess'. Emma had been the first girl born into the family since her mother's own birth, and she came into the world having two older brothers. How blessed were her parents.

The boys were older than their sister by eight and ten years and consequently had little time for her. She didn't play football or cricket and generally was a nuisance. Emma didn't mind. She spent a lot of time on her own, made up her own games, told all of her thoughts to Rag Doll. Emma was a lonely child. She didn't feel like the 'favourite girl 'or the 'little princess' and she carried on burying her dolls in the garden.

When she reached ten or eleven years old, Emma lost what little interest she had in her dolls, her 'dead babies'. Even her one treasured rag doll was put with toys she had outgrown and consigned to a box in the loft.

Her mother remarked that 'surely Emma had more dolls than these?', but didn't ask or pursue the matter any further. Emma had always been a loner as a child so her mother couldn't blame contemporaries for taking a fancy to her toys and removing them. Maybe Emma was forgetful and had left them on shopping trips or holidays, - yes, that must be it. The thought whipped through Mrs Kemp's mind and was gone, forgotten; put to bed to join the long list of other thoughts that had whipped through Mrs Kemp's mind during Emma's childhood. After all, they were blessed parents, weren't they?

Emma wasn't an academic child. Her brothers had the brains, Emma was arty. Not only that, but Emma was artful. She had learned from an early age to hide things from her parents and the older she became the easier it was. Her parents stopped calling her their 'little princess'. Family stopped doting on her as their 'favourite girl'. Other babies had been born into the family, other girls. New cousins usurped this blessed child. Was she ever?

1959

Emma's transition from awkward teenager to stunning young woman was completed before she was twenty. Her brothers were married and settled. Don, the older brother had recently become a father. Born prematurely, his son Josh was six weeks old before he had been allowed home from the hospital. Don and his wife Charlotte were thrilled to show off their son, tiny scrap that he was. Both sets of grandparents were delighted, Emma was a devoted aunty, 'he's such a doll,' she remarked.

When Josh was eight months old Don and Charlotte celebrated their second wedding anniversary. Emma was of course, 'only too pleased to babysit.' When the proud parents returned from their evening out, Emma said Josh 'hadn't been a spot of trouble, he's slept right through.'

'He's supposed to be wakened for a feed. I told you,' Charlotte said, as she pulled away from Don and ran upstairs to the nursery. Emma looked at her brother, then getting her bag from the sofa she said,

'I'm sorry I'm not perfect enough for you both. Sorry for not doing a better job for the precious Josh.'

Don looked at his sister and then upstairs, Charlotte was calling, 'Don, he's fine, just fine.'

Charlotte stood on the landing with the child in her arms.

No one noticed Emma leave and nothing more was mentioned of that evening. Don and Charlotte didn't let Emma come again into their perfect world.

Four summers would pass before Emma left her parent's home for a flat in London. She had studied art at college and had managed to get a job in a London gallery. While at college she had a fling with one of her lecturers. It lasted beyond her final exams. He was married. Emma didn't mind. He could get a divorce, couldn't he?

With Emma in London, Geoff Carlisle thought he and his marriage would be safe. He was wrong. Three years after Emma had left her Surrey home, Geoff moved in with her. It took another two years before he eventually got a divorce. He and Emma set a wedding date for the following April.

1970

'Emma's marrying Geoff Carlisle. He's the art historian, written several books, appeared on T.V. as the 'expert' for an antiques programme. We're terribly thrilled.'

Emma's mother retold this tale over and over to anyone who would listen and to anyone who was a captive audience. Emma was thirty when she married, Geoff was fifty-five. Emma had said she wanted a family right away. Geoff was non committal. He had three children from his first marriage, twin sons and a daughter. The twins were twenty-seven, their sister twenty-three.

Emma was pregnant within six months.

'Hello, daddy,' she said to Geoff one evening when he returned home from a lecture tour. The response was not what Emma had expected. Geoff sat down, 'I didn't really expect this, not now. I hadn't considered you to be so serious about having children.'

'I thought you'd be delighted, or at least slightly pleased,' Emma shrieked.

'Emma, I told you from the start. I know it's not the right thing to say and definitely not the right time but everything we've done is wrong. I doubt we'll ever really be happy.'

'I'm having a baby,' Emma said and began to cry.

'It won't wash this time,' Geoff said.

'You don't know what you're saying,' Emma said.

The tears left her eyes in an instant. Geoff remained unmoved.

1971

Geoff remained distant, but as the due date approached he mellowed and was with Emma for the birth of their son, Jolyon. Emma and Geoff seemed to patch up their differences for a while after the birth of their son and to outsiders they seemed to live perfectly happy lives.

By the time Jolyon was six months old he had started to be quite sickly. He couldn't keep his food down and was losing weight.

'You should take him to the doctor, or at least the clinic. Let someone take a look at him. My other children weren't like this, it's not normal.'

'So you think I can't look after him, that's it isn't it? I can't be trusted to look after your son. I'm not as good a mother as Jackie was, say it, say it.'

'Calm down, Emma. It's our baby we're

talking about. I want what's best for him. I'm not comparing you.'

'No, and don't. I'll look after him, all right. It's just, I know he's special and he's so like a doll, especially when he's asleep. I like him then, when he's quiet.'

Geoff flashed a look at Emma.

'He's not supposed to be too quiet, Emma.'

Another month passed. Jolyon just wasn't thriving.

'If you won't take him to the doctor, ask your mum to call in. She'll have an idea.'

Emma wasn't thrilled at all by this and told Geoff 'not to worry, the baby was fine, and anyway I'm pregnant again.'

Geoff was due to go away again on a two month lecture tour in Europe.

'I'll cancel, stay here and look after you both, you and Jolyon.'

'No, you must go. I'll be fine. We'll all be fine,' Emma replied.

Geoff conceded.

The morning he was leaving Geoff kissed his son and said, 'daddy'll be back soon.'

He'd been gone three weeks when he was called back to attend Jolyon's funeral. His son had succumbed and died and Emma had never mentioned it. He'd 'phoned her every evening. He must've called on the day Jolyon died. Emma had never thought to mention the death of their son.

It was Emma's mother who broke the news to Geoff, 'unexplained' she said, 'a cot death'. Geoff was devastated. Emma failed to show any emotion.

‘She’s in shock, that’s what it is,’ her mother explained.

Geoff couldn’t explain it away so easily, particularly when Emma said,

‘Don’t be so morose, Geoff. We’ll have another baby soon. It’ll be fine, you’ll see.’

To Geoff it seemed impossible that a woman, a mother, could behave in this way. Their son, barely seven months old had just died. They had attended his funeral, his tiny white coffin not much bigger than a shoebox, and Emma seemed to have no thought for him.

1972

Charles, their second son was born healthy and weighing in at 9lbs 11oz.

‘We don’t have to worry about this chap,’ Geoff said, ‘he’s a real fighter.’

‘You think so?’ Emma said and smiled.

Charles was a fractious baby from the start. He didn’t feed well, cried a lot of the time and was impossible to settle. Emma was exhausted. Geoff tried to help his wife all he could. He was only lecturing now two half days a week. Being at home meant more time with Emma. It was a strain. She had never really grown up. He found her tiresome. If it wasn’t for Charles he would probably leave. Emma had been a terrible mistake.

Three months after Charles was born history started to repeat itself. He became sickly, unable to keep his food down and was losing weight. Geoff was concerned. He waited until Emma had gone out and contacted the doctor. He wanted to bring

Charles in for a check- up. He was alarmed when the receptionist told him that Mrs Carlisle had changed practice, for herself and the baby. They were no longer under their care, and no she couldn't tell him the practice they had transferred to.

'But I'm the baby's father, he said.

'I'm sorry, but I don't know that,' replied the receptionist, 'and it would be against confidentiality regulations for me to say any more without the knowledge of your wife.'

'What if his condition worsens?'

'There's always A and E,' she replied.

Emma was quite perky when she arrived home. Geoff was sitting in the lounge having a drink when she breezed in.

'How are my boys?' she asked.

'We're fine. I don't think Charles seems as sickly today.' Geoff was lying but he wanted to see Emma's reaction. Her face didn't give anything away, she just said, 'that's good.'

Two weeks later, Emma had to go out, 'meeting friends', she said. Geoff had agreed to stay at home with Charles. Charles wasn't improving and Geoff was worried. He waited until Emma had left the house and then took Charles off to the hospital. He was heartened when the staff told him there didn't seem to be any underlying condition but they were keeping him in overnight as a precaution. He was dehydrated. They would put him on a drip. He would soon recover.

Geoff returned home to be greeted by Emma.

'Where's Charles?' she demanded.

'The hospital, he'll be in overnight. He's

dehydrated, but nothing serious to worry about.'

'I hope you know what you've done,' she said, 'they've had three babies over the last six months taken from there. That hospital has no security as far as I can see. Anyone can get into the baby unit and the nursery. It's a nightmare.'

'I didn't know,' Geoff replied.

'Why should you?' Emma said, 'you're either teaching or locked up in your study writing art books. You pay very little attention to Charles or to me for that matter. I don't know why I married you. It was different before, I know that.'

'Different for both of us,' Geoff said, 'anyway we can collect him in the morning, but if you want I can take you there now, you could probably stay with him.'

'No need. He'll be fine I'm sure,' she replied.

He was. They were able to bring Charles home the following afternoon. The hospital wanted him back, just for a 'check' the following week.

Geoff made sure that Charles was feeding, sitting with Emma when he could to see for himself how much his son was taking on board. Emma hadn't fed either of their children herself, 'the thought of it,' she once said, 'disgusts me and I shan't be demeaned in that way'.

At his hospital visit Charles passed all the checks and pleased the hospital staff with a weight gain of 5oz. He was still small for his age and birth weight but he was making progress. Geoff would just have to keep a close eye on his wife and son from now on.

A week or two later the local paper was full of

the ‘missing babies’ Emma had mentioned. The police had been trying to keep a lid on it but worried parents had leaked the story to the press. In a couple of hours it would be on TV and by morning on the front page of every ‘National’. It seemed that all the babies were taken from the premature baby unit. Geoff put the paper down. He was thankful that his son had returned home safe and well.

1975

During the summer of 1975 Charles started playgroup. He was a boisterous three year old and loved being with the other children. Charles particularly liked Mrs Young, his group teacher and when Emma dropped him off each morning it was Mrs Young he ran to. Geoff always picked Charles up. He insisted it was to help his wife, give her some free time, secretly he didn’t entirely trust her.

In the school holidays Charles stayed with granny Kemp. It was a routine that had started following the death of Mr Kemp the previous year. Mrs Kemp looked forward to each ‘end of term’ and hoped to have Charles stay as often as he wanted.

‘Mum’s becoming frail, she won’t be able to cope with Charles much longer, not now he’s becoming bigger and wanting to be outside more.’

‘Your mum’s fine and she loves him being there. Don’t stop these little pleasures for her and Charles’.

‘It can’t last, that’s all I’m saying.’ Emma replied.

Josh, Don's son was now approaching sixteen. He didn't see anything of his aunty Emma or her family. There had been, he was told, a disagreement when he was young. No one told him more than that and he was never interested enough to ask.

1977

Mrs Kemp's frailty became more apparent. Her mind was wandering and it wasn't thought right to let Charles stay with her on his own anymore. It upset Charles that he couldn't 'look after granny'. Emma started to stay with her mother more often. She would cook her meals and stay over one or two nights a week. Mrs Kemp's condition deteriorated. She was admitted to hospital and remained in their care for two weeks. On December 27th she died peacefully in her sleep. Emma was with her when she died.

The funeral was to take place at the local church on the Friday, 6th January. Mrs Kemp would be interred with her husband. Don and Rick barely managed to acknowledge their sister.

'We'll all have to get together', Emma said. Rick remained tight lipped. Don remarked that the reading of the will would be soon enough.

The family home was on the market for an age, or so it seemed. It was about twelve months before everything was finally sorted out, a developer eventually getting planning permission for five houses.

1979

Following the sale of the property Emma felt

she could do no better than go her own way. She was a wealthy woman now, in her own right. In February of 1979 Emma and Geoff divorced. No other party was involved and it was all quite amicable. Emma was granted custody of Charles and Geoff had reasonable access. Emma stayed on in the marital home. Geoff, now approaching sixty-five was glad for the freedom that his divorce had brought him. Being married to Emma had been a strain. Now his time was his own. He rarely lectured anymore. He moved from central London and found himself a small flat in Towcester.

Emma wasn't lonely. She had a friend to talk to. Rag doll had been found during the clearing of the house. Emma came across the box of toys in the loft. She brought Rag doll home with her. Emma told Rag doll all the problems she had. The problems with her brothers, the problems she'd had with her parents, problems with her nephew, the problems with Geoff, Jolyon, and Charles. Rag doll always listened, never criticised. Rag doll understood.

Since the divorce Emma had been leading a pretty solitary existence. Charles enjoyed spending as much time as he could with his father and Emma didn't seem to mind.

Occasionally she would walk past her childhood home. The bulldozers had moved in and the house had been virtually demolished. Soon the building work would start. The gardens had yet to be cleared, but that wouldn't take long.

When the work started on the gardens it was only pieces of doll that were found at first. Some of the dolls were in boxes, others were just broken pieces wrapped in fragments of cloth. Further into the garden human remains were discovered, the remains of babies; young babies no more than weeks old. The area was sealed off. Work stopped. In total six infants were found. Emma and her brothers were interviewed by the police.

Tests on the remains proved that three of the babies were those that had been taken from the hospital the year Charles was born. On reading the report, Geoff went to his local police station and although they found his revelations interesting there was nothing more they could do. There was nothing to link Emma to the deaths, 'she's been questioned and eliminated from our enquiries' he was told, 'and burying plastic dolls is not an offence'.

Emma didn't seem to care much about anything anymore. She was becoming more of a recluse. She had Rag doll to talk to, she didn't need other company. Rag doll knew all her secrets and thoughts, and would never tell, never.

8 THE READING GROUP

For several weeks now Trevor had been attending the reading group at his local library. It ran for an hour, two-thirty until three-thirty pm, on a Thursday afternoon. Two or three short stories were read, and each discussed. Sometimes two librarians would share the task of reading between them; on other occasions there would be a 'read around' within the group, each member reading up to half a page before passing the book on for the next person to read. The 'read around' only tended to happen when more people attended. The average attendance had been seven, plus the librarians, and on occasions when ten or more was achieved, be prepared to read yourself! Of late the numbers had been steadily growing, and in these times of cuts, reduced hours and staffing, the rise in numbers was hailed a success.

Trevor didn't like reading aloud,

'I've not done this since I were a lad at school,'

he complained, but performed the task anyway. He didn't like the discussion part of the group either. He knew what he liked and THAT wasn't up for discussion – end of story.

Half way through the afternoon one or other of the librarians made tea and handed round biscuits. Trevor enjoyed this part of the afternoon. He enjoyed all the afternoon really, truth be known. He enjoyed the company and the meeting up with people who he considered to be his friends. Trevor you see was a lonely man. Recently retired he lived alone. Once, a long time ago there had been a 'Mrs Trevor', not anymore though.

The reading group had never been a group where members' shared their own thoughts for discussion, Trevor changed that. When the opportunity arose either because of the story or another member's throw away comment, Trevor would spout forth. Over the past few weeks other group members had learned of his time at military college, his ten years serving in the Royal Marines. His life as a boy growing up in Wiltshire – happy times, he had a blessed childhood. Then all that behind his life as a civil engineer and the countries he had visited. Trevor sometimes hinted at his life with 'Mrs Trevor', but apart from a 'hint' no one in the group knew anything.

Some members of the group actually looked forward to the library visit more to hear Trevor's stories than to hear the two or three short stories the librarians chose. Membership of the group soared as of news of 'Trevor's Tales' spread around the town. Trevor didn't disappoint either. As soon as possible he'd throw in another story from his past and have the group in thrall. The sessions sometimes ran over and it was getting to the point where only one short story was being discussed. What was being discussed wasn't what the group was set up for. The librarians who ran the sessions deliberated over what action to take. They had to get everything back on an even keel. It wasn't exactly form for an outsider to start running library activities. On the other hand, Trevor was a popular member of the group and he'd brought more members to the library, - they decided that whatever happened they were on a bit of a sticky wicket. They'd leave things for a while. Let things run their natural course. See where it all ended up. Maybe review things at the staff meeting.

The reading group met throughout the year with a break in August. They resumed on the second Thursday of September. Trevor was there at two- fifteen. He didn't want to be late. He enjoyed the celebrity that being part of the group brought him.

The first story up for discussion was one of love, loss and undying affection. The ladies in the group thought it was one of the better stories of its genre. Trevor didn't agree, '*women,*' he said '*were not to be trusted.*'

There were gasps from the group and many raised eyebrows from the ladies who wanted to know how he could have such disregard for one whole section of society.

'The school of life taught me many things,' Trevor said, 'that you can't trust women is just one of them.'

Miriam who usually sat quiet as a mouse, even during the discussion, was moved to speak.

'Trevor,' she said, 'I don't know what has happened to you at all in your relationships with women, or how you have come to the opinions you have, but until you make me believe differently I do not wish to be associated with this group any more. I come to the library to discuss short stories, not take part in '*Trevor's Tales*.' Now if you will excuse me, goodbye all,' and with that Miriam left.

Other ladies in the group carried on chatting as the two librarians tried to bring calm.

'I think we'll do the next one as a 'read around', there are enough of us,' one of them said.

Trevor said, 'Apologies one and all, come on, no hard feelings, eh?'

The read around began, one of the groups regular members read first, she began, ' Hazel was not a beauty, not by any classical standard. Her features were somewhat sharp and her lips thin, but it didn't seem to matter. What did matter was that men found her attractive and more than that …' Carol was interrupted by Trevor,

'Are you trying to be funny Carol? I thought this next story was a murder', and why have you chosen my wife's name, Hazel? You know what happened don't you?"

Carol stopped, stunned.

'Sorry Trevor, this is how the story begins, look,' she passed the book to him from the point where she had been reading. Trevor read the passage for himself. He looked up and looked around the rest of the group.

'I'm sorry. I think I should go home,' he said.

The next week Trevor was missing from the group, and the week after that, and so it went on. The group shrank to its original core. The librarians were worried,

'Does anyone know where Trevor lives?' they asked group members as they arrived. No one had a clue. The discussions were definitely less lively. No one could hold the groups attention like Trevor.

Miriam returned to the group just before Christmas. In another couple of weeks the group would break for the holiday. There was only one librarian on duty now. The group had shrunk to four, it didn't warrant two anymore.

'Please,' he said, 'if any of you see Trevor in town, do ask him to come back. Tell him he's missed.'

After tea and biscuits the group left, wishing each other Christmas greetings as they did so.

It was in the last few days before Christmas that Miriam thought she saw Trevor in the local coffee shop. He was sitting alone at a table by the window. She didn't want to get too close in case he saw her, but was it him? It was three o'clock. Did he go there every afternoon, she wondered, or just on a specific day? Men, she thought were creatures of habit; she would check after Christmas.

Miriam spent Christmas with her son and daughter in law. She didn't arrive back home until the 7th January. She missed the first meeting of the group. When she went the following week, Trevor still hadn't turned up and no one had seen him. Miriam didn't mention that she thought she'd seen him, she had plans.

For the next two weeks Miriam spent every free afternoon at the shopping arcade. It was Trevor she had seen, she was certain of that now. It seemed he only went for coffee on Wednesday.

The next week, Miriam went for coffee on Wednesday, arriving at the shop by two-thirty. She wanted to see Trevor as he came in and act surprised! Everything went as she thought. Trevor was as amazed to see her as she looked to see him.

'Trevor, you've been missed at the group, won't you come back?'

'Well, you've changed your tune. You were the one who left because of me!'

'I know, and I'm sorry. I acted rather hastily, but I've started going to the group again. Why don't you?'

'I'll think about it,' he said, and went to sit down with his coffee at the table by the window.

Miriam attended the next meeting of the group with a spring in her step. She wanted to let everyone know she had seen Trevor and spoken to him. Only three people bothered to attend, none of them Trevor.

The next Wednesday, Miriam went to the coffee shop again. She arrived as before at two-thirty, and waited. By the time it was four-thirty, and three coffees later Miriam had to leave. Trevor hadn't shown up and she couldn't possibly drink any more coffee.

March turned to April. Trevor never returned to the group. Miriam never saw him in the coffee shop again. The group remained at a constant four.

Maxine, a junior library assistant who had been given the job of chairing the group for the last few weeks, had some bad news for the members of the group who remained. The group would disband next week when the library closed for Easter, without more interest the group just wasn't viable.

The group said they understood and would make the most of the last two meetings. Miriam arrived home that afternoon and felt despondent. She enjoyed her Thursday afternoon out. It was a chance to chat and socialise for an hour – and it didn't cost anything. She sat in her house. It was just going dark outside. In the late spring shadows she thought she recognised a figure passing by – Trevor!

Miriam hurried to the door and called out,

'Trevor, have you a minute?'

Trevor didn't stop or turn around. Miriam grabbed her coat and bag and was off. As she hurried along the road, the thought of what she was doing suddenly hit home. She stopped on the pavement and went through things in her head. Keeping her eyes on Trevor she pulled herself up to her full height, (5'2") and followed him. Miriam was going to find out where Trevor lived.

'*Miriam is being stupid,*' she thought, but she did it anyway. Filled with new vigour, Miriam followed Trevor for about ten minutes, then he turned left into a side street. It was a part of the town Miriam wasn't familiar with even though it was just under a mile away from her house. She watched from the end of the street, not wanting to get too near to her 'prey'. He turned into a gate at the end of a cul de sac. Miriam noticed a 'For Sale' board in the garden. She hurried now, wanting to catch up to him, to tell him about the group. Miriam arrived at the gate as Trevor was turning his key in the lock. She stood at the gate.

'Hello Trevor, I didn't realise you lived here.' Trevor turned.

'Hello Miriam, have you been following me?'

'No Trevor, don't be silly. Just visiting a friend – then, well, I thought it was you. Are you keeping well?'

'Yes thank you.'

'I see you're moving.'

'Seems so.'

'I don't know if you know or not, but the group's closing. Not enough interest. It's our last meeting next week. I wish you'd come back. I feel awful about it. I've ruined everything for everybody.'

'That just about sums it up, Miriam.'

'Well, I've told you now. It's up to you.'

The next Thursday, there were the four members of the group plus Maxine.

'I think we'll just have one story and then we can spend the rest of the hour chatting, it being our last meeting. That's if it's all right with you,' she said.

The four looked at one and other and agreed.

Miriam was intently listening to the story when she was nudged by her neighbour.

‘Look’, she hissed.

Miriam looked up. Trevor was coming in to the library. He walked over to the group.

‘Mind if I join you,’ he said.

‘No, sit down,’ was the reply of the four.

Trevor sat. After the reading, the discussion began. Trevor didn’t say a dicky bird. Eventually Maxine said.

‘Anything to add Trevor?’

‘Not about the story, no, but I would like to say I did enjoy my visits here on a Thursday. I’m sorry some people found me irksome but it’s just my way I’m afraid. Miriam mentioned to me last week that this was to be the last meeting and I thought I should like to attend. I’m glad I have. I move in a couple of weeks. My house has been sold and I’m off to pastures new, but old as well. I’m returning to Wiltshire, the county where I grew up. I met my wife there, when we were both seventeen, that’s a long time ago now. Everything’s a long time ago now. That’s what comes with age I suppose. She was a real beauty. I loved her, she said she loved me. Then I found out an awful truth, she loved someone else. Everything between us was false. She was playing a game, acting out a part. Sorry Miriam, but you can’t trust women.’

Maxine looked round, ‘shall we have tea now?’ she asked, trying to lift the discussion to a brighter plane.

‘Not for me,’ Trevor said, ‘I’d best be going.’

‘What happened to your wife?’ Miriam asked.

‘Dead. Killed in a car accident nearly forty years ago. She was leaving me. I didn’t want to blame her even then, but for years I asked myself, '*why*'?'. You see, I thought we were happy. I was. I just assumed …' His voice trailed off.

Trevor slapped his hands down onto his knees.

'I'll be off then,' he said, and stood up, 'It was good knowing you all. Bye.'

With that Trevor left. No one asked if he would keep in touch or visit occasionally.

Maxine passed round the tea and biscuits. End of discussion.

9 THE LITTLE BLACK DRESS

July 1999

Christine and her daughter Amelia were busy clearing the cottage where Christine's mother Charlotte, had lived. Charlotte's funeral had taken place a month ago but Christine had been putting off this final task.

'We'll start upstairs,' Christine said, 'you can go through the wardrobe in Gran's room.'

'On my own?'

'Yes, on your own. I just want to go and get some milk and coffee.'

'I'll make a drink Amelia. Are you ok?'

'Fine, mum. I've found the most marvellous dress. It fits me perfectly.' Amelia came down the stairs with me on. I must admit it was good to see the light of day after so long.

'What do you think mum, would Gran mind if I

had this?'

'No. You have it. It looks lovely on you.'

When Charlotte bought me in the summer of 1935 she was just nineteen years old. She had me 'laid aside' for six weeks, the maximum that 'Madame Leonie' would allow.

Charlotte collected me on Saturday the 20th July. She would wear me at her first cocktail party. We didn't know then where we would be in a few years time or that so much could happen. It's perhaps better that life is like this otherwise we may not get to enjoy our happinesses – not to the extent we should. And that's what the summer of 1935 was – happy.

Charlotte worked all week at a firm of solicitors in Buckingham town centre. She had been with them since she matriculated from the Latin school. She had hopes of becoming a fully fledged legal secretary and working for Mr John Marsden, the senior partner of Goldrick and Kelly, (Messrs Goldrick and Kelly being long since deceased).

Mr Marsden was only thirty-seven, but to Charlotte seemed very old. He lived for his work and his work only. The rest of the world could go its own sweet way, and it did, and Mr John Marsden never noticed a thing.

Charlotte worked until 1pm. on Saturdays. Madame Leonie closed for lunch between one and two pm, so Charlotte killed time by taking lunch in the park before she collected me. Me, being black silk georgette with a high waist, calf length and flowing hemline. The turn back of my asymmetric neckline was lined with gold coloured satin, as were the cuffs. The sleeves stopped just below the elbow.

When Charlotte tried me on that afternoon, Madame Leonie herself said how wonderful she looked. Madame Leonie was in fact Marjorie Pargeter. She was only forty-five years old and had opened her shop six years ago following the death of her husband and decided then that 'Madame Leonie' was the perfect name for her fashion empire. (She had a fancy that being dark she could pass for French.) She had moved to the town from Winslow and no one in Buckingham knew her as Marjorie, they always greeted her with 'Good morning Madame Leonie,' and it did Marjorie's heart good.

'Is the dress for a special occasion?' Madame Leonie asked.

'I work at Goldrick and Kelly and it's our summer cocktail party. Everyone's going, well staff that is, and some clients ...' her voice trailed off.

'Ah, you'll outshine everyone there with your choice.'

'I hope, well what I mean is, I hope I do everything right.'

'You can't fail. Don't be nervous, enjoy the occasion and smile a lot. It helps immensely.'

Charlotte smiled. She found the last remark rather amusing.

'There, that's it! You have a perfect smile!'

'Now let me see,' said Madame Leonie taking a book from a drawer by the till,

'Yes, here we are, the dress cost £1. 17s 6d,

less ten shillings deposit that's just £1.7s 6d to pay please.'

Charlotte took the money from her purse and paid.

'Let me know how you get on,' Madame Leonie said as Charlotte left the shop.

'Come on then, let's see you in all your finery.' Charlotte's mother was holding court at their cottage.

'Dad, dad, put your paper down and look at Charlotte, she's a picture.'

Dad did as he was told.

'What do you think, dad?'

'Just what your mother said Charlotte, you look a picture.'

Charlotte kissed them both and went off, 'I'll be home between ten and eleven, don't worry.'

Charlotte met up with the other girls from the office. They were older than Charlotte, only a few years, but Charlotte thought they were far superior. Jane was twenty-three and next year would be marrying her childhood sweetheart, Tom. Grace was twenty-five and worried about being 'left on the shelf', but thought Charlotte, there was no chance of that, she was far too pretty. Evelyn was just twenty-one, a dark beauty who seemed to know everything. In charge of this young brood was Miss Clarke, a plump, grey haired be-spectacled spinster. Miss Clarke was wearing what would be known as 'Sunday best', she had dressed up, but not so much as the girls for the occasion. Together they walked down to the meadow. A marquee had been set up close to the river's edge and Chinese lanterns lit the pathway. It was a sight Charlotte was never to forget. Inside the marquee a band played and there was a dance floor. There were tables laden with hot and cold finger food, hot cheese puffs, cocktail sausages and sausage rolls and Charlotte's favourite, chicken livers in bacon blankets! Charlotte also discovered a liking that night for smoked salmon canapés and celery stuffed with crabmeat. She gave the caviar a miss, that was one treat too many as far as she was concerned. There was a good assortment of bite sized fancy cakes and of course the cocktails. Charlotte was more amazed by their names. She knew Martini of course, but then *'Rosebud'* and '*The Doctor'*, (which she didn't try) and then something everyone seemed to be having, *'Pimm's Cup'*. Miss Clarke said that this was a particular favourite of hers in hot weather and tonight was particularly hot.

'You know you have the first dance with Mr John,' Evelyn said.

Charlotte blushed, 'Me?'

'Yes, you. You're the junior member of staff. It's tradition. I'm just glad you joined us. I've been dancing with him for the last three years. It's awful, he can't dance.'

'You're joking,' Charlotte said.

Charlotte was nervous and shaking when Mr John came over to her.

'Miss Stanton, I believe the pleasure is mine?'

Charlotte gawped at him, red faced. Evelyn nudged her, 'Go on Charlotte, time to dance.'

Charlotte turned and smiled at her companions

and headed for the dance floor with Mr John Marsden. The first dance was a fox trot and contrary to what Evelyn had said Charlotte thought he danced rather well for an old man.

'Are you enjoying working with us, Miss Stanton?'

Charlotte smiled and nodded.

'I see,' he replied.

'Are you enjoying yourself this evening?'

Charlotte smiled and nodded again.

'You don't say much do you Charlotte?' he said, smiling.

Charlotte smiled and shook her head.

Evelyn was watching from her seat.

'Well, what do you know,' she said, 'old Mr John's smiling.'

At ten o'clock the evening came to a close. The girls and Miss Clarke walked to the centre of town together and then went their separate ways. Charlotte was full of it the next day and it was all her parents heard every time she spoke.

The year passed quickly and I was put away until Christmas. Christmas day would be Charlotte's twentieth birthday. She would be working until two pm. on Christmas Eve. Miss Clarke was leaving at eleven am. She was spending Christmas with her brother. He had three young boys and she had gifts for them all. A car for Tom, the eldest, a wooden fort for David, and a drum for Christopher, and she laughingly told the girls, 'I've bought them a lot of chocolate, but it's only once a year.'

Miss Clarke's brother was a lawyer in

Aylesbury and would be collecting his sister in his new Crossley Regis Sports saloon. It was brown and cream and her brother had told her, '*she does twenty-two miles to the gallon.*' That hadn't meant a lot to Miss Clarke. She just knew that it was fourteen miles to Aylesbury and that the round trip would take at least two gallons of petrol. Miss Clarke was so happy that morning.

'Come across to the window and I'll wave to you from the car.' she said.

It was almost two o'clock. The girls were getting ready to leave the office. Mr John came through from his office, 'Miss Stanton, would you mind coming through to the office please?'

Charlotte blushed. The other girls looked at one and other, 'Wonder what she's done?' Evelyn said.

Charlotte was in the office no more than a few minutes. When she came out she was carrying a gent's umbrella and smiling. 'What's that?' Jane said, then 'And what happened?'

Charlotte laughed. 'I was worried, but Mr John said he knew that my father was a gent's hairdresser and that he repaired umbrellas and as this is his favourite, he wondered if my dad could repair it over the Christmas holiday.'

'He wants your dad to fix his umbrella?' Grace said.

'Yes,' Charlotte replied, 'and he said we could all go now and he'll see us in the New Year.'

'But we haven't had our Christmas present. We always get a Christmas present. A '*thank you*' he calls it, for all our work through the year.'

'Well I don't know about that,' Charlotte

replied, 'but I'm going home, it's almost Christmas.'

I came out on Christmas day and I must say Charlotte looked good. She had teamed me with a black lace stole, hand decorated with black and white iridescent seed pearls.

Whether Mr John had forgotten or not, we'll never know but what we do know is that Charlotte enjoyed Christmas and her birthday. Her father even enjoyed repairing Mr John's umbrella. Mr Stanton proclaimed it was a real treat to repair an umbrella made by 'Fox's of London' as they were just about the best a man could own.

1936 dawned and soon it was back to the familiar territory of Goldrick and Kelly. Evelyn, Grace and Jane were at the office when Charlotte arrived.

'Oh,' said Jane, 'you're here. Mr John said we're all to go through to the office when you arrived.'

The four girls went through to the office where Mr John sat behind a large oak desk.

'Please sit down girls. I've got some news and I want to tell you all together. Now first, some very sad and shocking news,' Mr John didn't look at any of them, just stared down at his desk as he spoke, 'I'm sorry to have to tell you that Miss Clarke is no longer with us. Travelling to her brother's on Christmas Eve, Miss Clarke was involved in an accident. We're not sure exactly what happened, we think the car may have had a puncture and the tyre needed changing. Miss Clarke attempted to assist her brother and in doing so stepped into the path of another vehicle. Her mind was obviously on other matters. Witnesses say she just stepped out into the road without looking, the driver hadn't a chance of stopping,' he paused then carried on, 'I know we shall all miss her.'

Charlotte and Grace began to cry.

Mr John continued, 'my next news is on a happier note. I shall be marrying in October and while I'm honeymooning my brother Charles will be taking over my responsibilities here. I know you will enjoy working for him as you do for me. That is all girls, you may now carry on.'

They returned to the office and began their morning's work.

'I hope his wedding doesn't clash with mine,' Jane said, 'I don't want to miss the invitation. We'll get one, won't we?'

'No,' Evelyn answered bluntly. 'We're staff aren't we, why should we get an invite; no more than you'd invite Mr John to yours, and any way your wedding's in April. I'm right aren't I?'

The next time I was worn was for Jane's wedding. It was April 1936. Charlotte changed the colour of the lining to a bright fuchsia pink and wore a fuchsia plate hat and fuchsia shoes. She carried cream lace gloves. It was a beautiful day and Jane and Tom made a lovely couple. Jane gave up work and became a village housewife, moving with Tom to a cottage in Foscott. Jane's family thought she could have done better, but nevertheless were still glad to see their daughter married and happy.

Jane and Tom's day of sunshine and happiness was in stark contrast to Mr John's own wedding day. Saturday, October 10th. The storms that had been prevalent for most of that month persisted and that October day dawned with high winds and torrential rain. Three o'clock, the time of the wedding, and the weather hadn't changed. It was an awful day, and Evelyn was right, the staff weren't invited.

Monday October 13th arrived, still stormy, and with it arrived Mr Charles Marsden, Mr John's younger brother. He was younger than Mr John by some ten years and as unlike his older sibling as any man could be. Evelyn took a shine to him at once,

'He's dishy, not like the other one,' she said.

'I don't like him.' Charlotte replied.

Friday December 25th 1936. Charlotte's twenty-first birthday. Charlotte wore me again, still the fuchsia contrast to neck and cuffs, but this time set off with a string of pearls. A twenty-first present from her parents.

Sunday 14th February 1937. A Valentine dance at the Town Hall. It was wet. A true 'February fill dyke'. Fashion dictated a rising hem line. Charlotte shortened me to just below the knee and added a large dress clip to one side of the neckline. I loved being dressed up! Well, doesn't every little black dress!

December 1937. I'm going to have two outings this month, my first, Saturday 4th December when

Evelyn marries Mr Charles. Can you believe it?

Mr John has been back since the beginning of March, but the thing is since he's been back he doesn't seem to pay so much attention to the business. All he seems to think about is home and Sarah. Maybe that's as it should be. Sarah does like to spend though and if it's not fancy things for the house it's the latest fashions from 'Madame Leonie'. Madame Leonie is making hay while the sun shines and orders in all the latest fashions for Sarah from Paris and London.

Evelyn and Charles married at St. Edmund's in Moreton. Evelyn looked wonderful in a dress of ivory lace and full veil and train. Charlotte wore me and a lovely silver fox stole, (borrowed from mum) and a matching hat.

Christmas 1937, Charlotte was twenty-two years old. It was a Saturday. Charlotte walked to Foscott to visit Jane and Tom after church. Their cottage was decorated for Christmas and in the corner of the room was a small tree.

'Tom brought it home last night and we decorated it together, Phoebe watched from her pram.'

'It's beautiful, your home, everything. You're lucky Jane.'

She took a little package from her bag, 'it's a gift for Phoebe.'

April 1938. The cocktail party was going to be in April this year. The brothers had decided to bring the party forward as the weather had been so unbelievably dry. Since February there had been very little rain.

April 16th, Saturday. Charlotte was looking forward to the party. The setting, down by the river was always perfect. Charlotte didn't think there was anything to quite match the view as you walked across the meadow and the marquee came into sight with its twinkling fairy lights and Chinese lanterns against the backdrop of the river Ouse. It was quite magical.

Charlotte still liked me and I came out once more. She had tried a dress on at Madame Leonie's but the only difference was that this year's dress had a contrasting bow that fell from just below the bust line, the tails of the bow stopping just above the knee. Charlotte thought she could make a bow similar from some of the fuchsia satin she had left over. I was perfect for the cocktail party.

It was busy at the office, with only Charlotte and Grace to do the work. It seemed as if times that were tough were just going to get tougher. All the news was dominated by Germany and their chancellor, Herr Hitler. It appeared he wasn't the most popular man in Europe. Charlotte didn't really understand or discuss politics much but she did feel un-easy whenever he was mentioned. Grace had said she might move away, take a chance on a job in London, 'more chance of a wealthy husband there' she'd said.

Charlotte wasn't so sure, 'I'd rather be happy,' she replied.

Before Christmas that year, on Tuesday

December 6th, Alexandra Felicity Marsden was born. The first child of Mr John and Sarah. 'Mother and baby are in excellent health,' Mr John announced later that day.

Charlotte and Grace bought a small pink hairbrush and comb for the baby. They passed it on via Mr Charles, Mr John having left the office after making the announcement and not returning to work after that. No one knew why. That is to say Charlotte and Grace didn't know why. They would find out later in the New Year.

Evelyn was in the office waiting for them when they returned to work after the Christmas holiday.

'Happy New Year, stranger,' Charlotte said.

Grace added, 'Charles making you work is he?'

'No, but he wants me to make an announcement to you. Could you come through to the office, please? I honestly don't know why Charles thinks I'll be any better at this than he would, but here goes, I've said I'll do it and I will. I'm afraid Mr John will not be returning, ever. None of us knew but he had enormous debts – gambling, sometimes with the firm's money. We can carry on. It'll be tough but Charles thinks we can sort everything out.'

'Where's Mr John, and his family?' Charlotte asked.

'They've moved to London. He's still a fine lawyer and a university friend has offered him work- provided he turns his life around. There's a flat with the job and so Sarah and Alexandra will be secure'

'I can't believe Mr John would do such a thing.

He lived for his work, it was his life,' Grace said.

'We were all shocked but sometimes it seems you never really know a person.'

Grace and Charlotte carried on discussing the revelation from Evelyn and still found it hard to take in. Grace said she was 'more determined than ever to make the move to London.'

January 1939.

The whole country was hit by heavy snow fall. It really was a bleak winter and one of the coldest for many years. Charlotte was turned twenty-three and she wondered if she'd get another year out of me. Madame Leonie was still serving the great and the good of Buckingham but new fashions were slow to move, people seemed wary of buying.

'I might have to close if people don't spend with me,' she declared to Charlotte one day. 'You'll have to ask for a raise and then you can spend it with me.'

After the snow and the cold of winter, May was a welcome release. It was bright and sunny. The cocktail party that had always taken place in a marquee by the river was cancelled.

'I'm sorry, Charlotte, Grace, but we just can't do it this year. I really am sorry,' Evelyn told them, Charles having persuaded her once more to break bad news.

'Great,' Grace said when she was speaking to Charlotte later on, 'We have to work every hour because there's just the two of us, and now, no party! I don't believe it's that bad, and it's all the fault of that Mr John. We'd be finished if we'd gambled away the firm's money but he gets a second chance. All right for some.'

'Don't be like that Grace. We can still do something. The Town Hall has started tea dances on a Sunday afternoon. There's one in a couple of weeks, May 14th.'

'A tea dance, do you mean it, really?' Grace asked with more than a hint of sarcasm in her voice.

'Yes, come on, it'll be fun.'

For this next event Charlotte altered me slightly. She made the tails on the bow shorter and shortened the sleeve to just above the elbow. I was quite impressed myself, after all this was my fourth year.

The tea dance was a great success, for Grace anyway. She would be twenty-nine in August and was feeling ever so slightly old. She thought she may turn into another Miss Clarke, and the thought of that terrified her. Grace and Charlotte had a couple of dances – albeit with each other and were sitting down when in through the door walked, 'Mr Right', Grace said.

'What?' asked Charlotte.

'I've just seen my future husband.'

'How can you say that?'

'Because I'm nearly twenty-nine and don't want to be single any more, tell you what, we'll dance the next dance together, head his way and bump into him. After that Charlotte, you can leave the rest to me.'

Grace's plan worked. Charlotte left it to her and in July Grace married Mr Edward Stiller at St. Leonard's church, Foscott. Grace looked a picture in ivory satin, Edward seemed rather nervous.

Charlotte wore me with the hat and accessories she'd worn for Jane's wedding. Jane brought two year old Phoebe along to watch and throw rose petals as the happy couple left the church.

With Grace married there was only Charlotte left working at Goldrick and Kelly. Mr Charles gave her a pay rise, an increase of 9d a week. She was now earning £1 15s 3d a week, she felt rich! She decided to save the 9d and see how much she could put aside.

Charlotte worked long hours, some nights not finishing until seven pm. Her parents worried that she might be doing too much. She told them not to worry, there were bigger things looming. Her father agreed with her, which only gave her mother more to worry about.

I didn't think I'd get another outing, not before Christmas at any rate and as it was Charlotte had given me more alterations than should be allowed. Madame Leonie continued to trade but as the weeks went by people were becoming more mindful of the bigger picture emerging in Europe, particularly where Herr Hitler was concerned. There were mutterings of war.

August was a month of mixed weather although occasionally there were days of un-broken sunshine. Charlotte spent some of her free time in the meadow by the river. Here everything seemed peaceful. There were no problems. She remembered her first party at Goldrick and Kelly. How she had felt when she saw the marquee for the first time, dancing with Mr John, the nervousness and then the relief when it was done. What happy times they had been!

It was on Sunday 3rd September that the Prime Minister, Mr Neville Chamberlain announced to the country that we were at war with Germany. All of a sudden there was a feeling of intensity in the town as people prepared for whatever was ahead.

The young men of the town who were already members of the Territorial Army were called up and taken for training to Aylesbury, some eventually going off to serve with the Northants Yeomanry. Charlotte worried about her dad, would he go? What would her mother do? Her dad was an A.R.P. warden and safe for the moment. He wasn't worried, 'We've been practising since March last year,' he said, 'let's get on with it.'

On Monday 4th September when Charlotte turned up for work it was to be told that the firm would be closing, but all being well, and if the war was over by Christmas then things would return to normal. Mr Charles had turned out to be quite 'a good egg', Charlotte thought, and remembered how at first she hadn't liked him. He explained to Charlotte that their case load would be taken over by Beale and Bowker who also had an office in town. As Mr Beale was well into his sixties he wouldn't be called upon to serve in the armed forces so was able to carry on practising.

Mr Charles would be going to join his old regiment, the Queens Own Oxfordshire Hussars. He said he was 'looking forward to it'. Charlotte doubted this. What was there to look forward to in war?

By the end of September Mr Charles had gone to join his regiment. Mr John, Sarah and Alexandra had returned from London. They rented a house on the Winslow Road. Alexandra was nearly ten months old, a lovely baby.

Mr John had sorted himself out while in London and there was no mention at all of his previous problems. Within weeks of his return he too had gone to join up. Mr John wasn't a military man like his younger brother, but wanted to do his 'bit'. The fact that Mr Charles had already re-joined his regiment meant he felt under pressure and Mr John didn't want to let anyone down.

December that year was cold and heavy snow lay all around. Buckingham wasn't the same. Many of the young men had left the town and gone off to serve their country. Charlotte felt miserable. She didn't know what the New Year would bring. She hoped peace, but who could tell?

December 6th was Alexandra's first birthday. Her daddy wasn't there to celebrate with her. Charlotte took her a small rag book by way of a present. Sarah was pleased to see Charlotte, they didn't get many visitors and she said she 'didn't know when John would be home'.

'I thought everyone would be home for Christmas,' Charlotte said, and then wondered as she spoke the words whether she really believed them.

'I doubt it,' said Sarah, 'didn't they say the same thing last time.'

Christmas came, Charlotte was celebrating her

twenty-fourth birthday, although the way things were, birthdays and Christmas didn't seem to warrant much celebration somehow.

Charlotte went to church with her mother. Her father said he would leave the 'church thing to them'. He was not a religious man. Charlotte smiled at her mother.

'He doesn't have to be a religious man mum. He's a good man, that's what counts.'

When Charlotte and her mother returned from church it was to be greeted with some bad news. Mr John was dead. He had taken his own life sometime around the 18th December, hanged himself in woods near to Brackley.

'I never took him for a military man,' Charlotte's father said, 'not like Mr Charles, anyway, sad news whatever the reason.'

'Who told you?' Charlotte asked.

'Peachy from the Post Office. He came round just after you'd left.'

'Are you sure he's got it right dad? You know he's worse than a woman for gossip.'

'He's right, Charlotte.'

And he was. There was memorial service at St Peter and St Paul in Buckingham in January. I came out again, minus bows and cuffs and neckline of fuchsia.

When Charlotte returned from church I was hung up in her wardrobe and never worn again, until now, when Amelia saw me and tried me on.

10 WHAT IS WAR?

He looked right and then left before continuing forward. He had to be away from this place, this horror they called war. But wasn't here where he'd wanted to be, fighting? It would be exciting, wouldn't it? The reality was different. Lice ridden uniforms, food not fit even for pigs, and mud. Mud and barbed wire as far as the eye could see. No Man's Land. A smile pinched at his lips. Yes. This was almost funny, comical. It would be something to tell his mother, later.

He was off again, forward; every step a step nearer home. Every day a day nearer War's End. It had to be, didn't it? He thought of each day as this, and then questioned the thought almost as soon as it had entered his head. Out here, you lost all sense of reason. You followed orders. Everybody did. You might question to your comrades, but you never questioned an officer. You just '*did*' whatever it was.

He was seventeen; he didn't want to be here,

not now he knew what war was. Not now he'd seen friends killed; not now he'd killed.

The air was full of smoke from artillery and mortar fire and the mud clung to him; hugged him in a tight, unbearable hold.

Suddenly, there was an almighty bang to the back of him, left side. He dropped down, hit the earth with a thud, and the surrounding mud splashed upwards. He gasped for air and took in mud. His lungs couldn't cough it up. He was choking. Turning his head upward he took a breath and coughed. This time it was all right; he cleared his lungs, but then saw the bright red spray. He'd been hit.

Closing his eyes he thought of home and of his parents. He pictured them the last time he'd seen them; waving as he walked up the path to be a soldier. His mother had said, *'Take care'.*

But war was a race against time, and he'd just lost.

11 HETTIE AND MR EVANS

Mr.Frederick Evans spent hours on his car. It was his pride and joy. He waxed and polished the bodywork, he polished the chrome until it was like a mirror. His wife watched him from the lounge window. Joyce was stopped in her observations by the sound of the 'phone ringing. She went through to the hall. Joyce couldn't watch from there, the glass to the front door was frosted.

'871592' she said.

'It's only me, Joyce. Thought I'd 'phone for a chat.'

'Hello mum, dad out?'

'No, he's having a lie down. It's his legs you know, they're still not right.'

There was silence.

'Joyce, are you there?'

Joyce was trying to observe Fred.

'Sorry mum. Dad out then?'

'Climbing Kilamanjaro.'

'Mum.'

'Well you're not listening. I don't know why I bother, I really don't.'

'Mum.'

'Don't 'mum' me my girl. Where's Fred?'

'Outside. Polishing Hettie.'

'He's got a fancy woman.'

'Mum, have you been drinking?'

'No, listen. He's been seen in town. Mabel Jackson told me. He's not trying to hide it.

It's been going on for months. She heard it from Emmie Baker.'

'Who are these people?'

'Friends of mine.'

'They don't sound like friends to me.'

'They've been round to see me today.'

'That's nice of them,' Joyce replied'

'You've gone quiet Joyce,' her mother said.'

'It's a lot to take in?'

'Will you leave him?'

'One step at a time mother. Who is the mystery woman anyway?'

'Mabel didn't say and Emmie wouldn't divulge much at all. So, no, I don't know.'

Frederick Evans came in while his wife was still on the 'phone.

'Who's calling?' he mouthed.

'Mum,' came back the silent reply.

He smiled, 'give her my love. I'm off to get washed and changed.'

'Are you there, Joyce?'

'Yes mum. Fred's just come in. He sends his love.'

'The cheek of it,' her mother said.

'Did you learn any actual facts from your friends?'

'Only that he's fed up with you and wanted something a little younger.'

'Mum.'

'It's true Joyce. I can hardly believe it myself, but that's what's been heard.'

'Thanks mum. I'll go now if you don't mind. I've a lot to think about.'

Fred came into the lounge to find his wife sitting looking at a blank television screen.

'You don't look well at all, love. Mum given you bad news?'

'Of sorts.'

'Not another funeral?'

'Not yet,' Joyce replied.

'What do you mean?'

'It doesn't matter. It was a private conversation between me and my mother.'

Frederick Evans didn't like it when his wife was in the mood for strange conversations. He never knew what to say.

'Shall I make you a cup of tea, love?'

'Oh, fine yes! That's your answer to everything - a cup of tea!'

Fred paused momentarily and moistened his lips. Suddenly his mouth had become dry, his head hot. He knew that whatever he said it would be wrong and that something was definitely his fault.

'Does that mean you'd like a drink Joyce?'

Joyce stood up.

'No,' she shouted, 'I do not want tea. I'm going out.'

A couple of minutes later Fred heard the front door open and then close. Joyce had gone. He went into the kitchen and brewed up. He couldn't think why she was so angry. Fred went into the garden. He felt the need for fresh air. Their neighbour Cyril was busy tending his vegetables. He stopped and looked over the fence.

'Are you in the doghouse, too?'

'I think so, though I don't know why,' Fred replied. 'You?'

'I'm always there,' Cyril answered. 'But I know why. That's the difference between us Fred.'

'And why are you in the doghouse?' Fred enquired.

'I married my Doris. It's as simple as that, but women love to talk so, leave them alone and they come round. You should try it Fred.'

'I will, as soon as Joyce comes home.'

Fred went back inside. It was twenty past four. He reckoned that Joyce would be back soon. He couldn't understand her. Perhaps he never would. Perhaps all women were like this, difficult to understand. He would suggest they went out for the evening. They hadn't been out in ages. Fred smiled, '*Yes, that would do the trick. That would smooth over whatever had annoyed her*'.

At half past nine that evening Joyce had not returned. The smile had gone from Fred's face, he ate alone. At ten o'clock Fred 'phoned Joyce's mum. He had worried whether it was too late to 'phone someone who was turned eighty. He also worried that it was too late to call his mother in law. Of the two worries the latter worried him more.

‘Hello, 574689.’

‘Mother, it’s Fred. I’ve not disturbed you have I?’

‘Yes, but carry on now you’re here.’

‘Great’, Fred thought, then he said, ‘Joyce was coming to visit you but she’s not arrived home yet. Is everything all right?’

Fred knew he was lying but hoped it wasn’t obvious.

‘No, she’s not here.’ Mary knew she was lying but didn’t care.

Fred replied, ‘I’ll call her mobile. Goodnight then.’

‘Goodnight Fred.’

As soon as she came off the ‘phone Mary went straight into the next bedroom,

‘Are you awake, Joyce? He’s ‘phoned. I told him you weren’t here. He’s going to ring your mobile. I should turn it off if I were you.’

‘Mum, you should’ve said I was here.’

‘You didn’t.’

Fred called Joyce’s mobile. It went straight to voice mail. He didn’t leave a message. Sitting on his own he began thinking, thinking about Hettie and Joyce. When they were first married they’d gone off to rallies with Hettie. Joyce seemed to like her then and would often help with the polishing. Lately things had gone a bit downhill, but not so much that she would leave him? Alf at the garage had often remarked how he’d love to get his hands on Hettie and Fred had always said no, but last week Alf had made an offer that Fred didn’t want to refuse. It had the potential to set him up for his retirement, maybe an early or semi retirement. All this just from letting Hettie go. All this even when he had bought a new car, (second hand, of course) that he and Joyce could go places in. Anyway, first he had to find out where Joyce was and get her back.

The next morning Fred had to get his own breakfast. This was a rarity. The only time he'd done this before was when Joyce was in hospital when the twins were born. This wasn't right. Joyce should be here with him. Maybe this was how Joyce felt when he went off with Hettie. Anyway that would soon be over.

Fred went out to the garage. Hettie was beautiful. He'd done a good job of polishing her this weekend. Alf wouldn't have any complaints. Her burgundy paintwork was gleaming, her tan interior leather beyond compare. Hettie was no ordinary car, she was a 1948 Jaguar mark V, three position drop head coupe.

Fred looked at his watch. It was nine o'clock. He tried Joyce's mobile again. It went straight to voice mail. This time Fred left a message. He asked Joyce where she was and told her he was worried. Fred put the 'phone down and waited. At ten past ten the 'phone rang. It was Phil, his son. Phil noted the dejection in his father's voice.

'Dad, are you ok? You sound odd.

'Your mum stayed out last night, I don't know where she is.'

'Dad, why didn't you 'phone? Does Chris know?'

'No. No one knows except your Gran. I've left

mum a message. I just hope she checks her 'phone.'

'Dad, I'll 'phone Chris, get him to come home. We can be with you in a couple of hours.'

'No. Stay where you are. I'll let you know this afternoon what's happening. It's no use all being worried.'

'I'll 'phone Chris and let him know.'

'OK. Anyway Phil, why did you 'phone?'

'Nothing dad. It doesn't matter.'

Fred sat down and wondered what he should do next. Should he wait or should he try Joyce's mobile again. It was a quarter to eleven. He 'phoned Mary.

'Hello mum, it's Fred. Just wondered if you'd heard from Joyce'

'No, nothing. You?'

'Nothing. I'll try her mobile. I have left a message but I'll try again. Thanks Mary, bye.'

Fred sat down. He knew Mary wasn't telling the whole truth. She was too calm when he'd said that he hadn't heard from Joyce. Anyone, a mother particularly, would have been worried.

He 'phoned Phil and asked him to call his mother's mobile and then 'phone him back, let him know where she was. He already had a suspicion.

'Dad, your guess was right. Mum's at Gran's. I had to tell a few white lies but at least you know she's all right.'

Fred got straight on the 'phone. He'd decided to do something that would be considered romantic. He would send flowers to his wife. He had done this before they were married. He had proposed to her via the card on the flowers twenty-eight years ago.

It was worth a try.

Fred ordered a bouquet that MUST contain Singapore orchids, white roses and lots of asparagus fern. They were to be sent to Joyce Evans at 29, Lower Crescent.

'The card', the assistant asked, 'what would you like on the card?'

Fred replied, 'Joyce, let's run away together.'

'Lovely,' the assistant replied.

'I hope so,' Fred said.

Back in the house Fred put on a shirt and tie and his grey pinstripe suit. He looked at the clock, it was eleven forty-five. The flowers should be arriving about now. He got Hettie out and set off for Mary's. At mid-day Fred was pulling up on the road outside his mother in law's house. He walked up to Mary's door and rang the bell.

'Is Joyce in?' he asked.

'No', she isn't. She's gone to the supermarket. I needed a few things.'

'If you'll ask me in, I'd like to wait for my wife.'

Begrudgingly Mary let Fred in.

'Has the florist been?' he asked.

'Yes.'

'Will Joyce be long?'

'I shouldn't think so.'

Fred smiled then said 'great'. He thought his mother in law might be mellowing. Her manner wasn't quite so aggressive. Even so, he wasn't offered a drink.

Joyce wasn't surprised to see Fred there when she returned. She'd seen Hettie parked outside.

'I'd better go and unpack this shopping,' she said.

'There's something for you in the kitchen,' Fred said, 'I hope you like it.'

Joyce smiled and carried on through the house. Her mother followed her. Fred waited.

As soon as she saw the flowers and the card Joyce came back through to the lounge.

'Fred, my wedding flowers, you've remembered.'

'I've never forgotten Joyce.'

Mary, who was standing behind Joyce 'Hmmphed'.

'Don't let him sweet talk you Joyce. Whatever he says he's still a man. I had to lay down the rules for your father. Ask him about his '*fancy woman*'.'

'What?' Fred questioned.

'Mum's right. It's the local gossip. You're leaving me. That's why I'm here, I need to think things through, but either way the flowers are lovely.'

'I don't know about the gossip but, it's all news to me. And to be honest Joyce, when would I have the time? You've said yourself, I'm always with Hettie. But I have got some news for you, Alf's having Hettie. By next weekend she'll be gone. He finally offered more than enough. I'll get a car we can both drive.'

'Really Fred?'

'Really.'

'She did get on my nerves you know.'

'I know, but let's get home. It's where you belong.'

‘Ok. But I want to ask mum something, about Emmie and Mabel. I think the gossip in the town’s coming from their direction.’

Mary gathered herself up and shrugged, ‘Well, it was all over town. It was common knowledge Fred Evans was moving on to pastures new.’

‘You got all this from Mabel and Emmie, I’d like to know where they heard it.’

‘I can’t divulge sources. They’d never tell me anything again.’

‘That mightn’t be a bad thing,’ Joyce replied.

Joyce picked up her flowers and took Fred’s arm.

‘Come on Fred, let’s go home,’ then added, ‘don’t go believing everything you hear mum, it could get you into serious trouble one day.’

Fred and Joyce travelled home in their separate cars, probably for the last time.

Mary shrugged again and then went in and checked on her husband. He was still resting his legs.

12 LIFTING

Wig Wam Toys had been selling to the people of Mardon for nearly fifty years. Unusual for an independent to be in business for so long these days but the McAllister family had a loyal clientele.

Mr McAllister was in the shop now. It was 1 pm., Wednesday. By now he would generally have put the 'closed' sign on the shop door and finished for lunch but Mrs Ham had called in to collect and pay for a bicycle for her grandson's birthday. He was five today and this was his first real bike. Mr McAllister smiled as he listened to the story. Mrs Ham was a frequent customer to the shop and had a habit of turning up at the last minute, shopping bag on arm, purse in hand and face flushed.

'I'm sorry for taking time off your lunch hour', she said, 'but it's the first chance I've had to get out. I've been so busy.'

Mr McAllister smiled and said that she wasn't to worry, that it was important that she get the bike home and ready for her grandson. Mrs Ham smiled gratefully at the shopkeeper.

Mr McAllister glanced at his watch. It was 1.05pm., not too bad. As he walked from the stockroom wheeling the bike through to the shop he noticed another customer. A young man, Mr McAllister had seen him in the shop before. He always seemed to be browsing.

'I've got the bike here. Would you just excuse me a moment Mrs Ham, I want to see where the young man has gone and if he needs any help.'

Mrs Ham smiled, but did not speak.

Mr. McAllister approached the young man who was busy looking at the rather large display of soft toys.

'Need any help there, young man?'

'No thanks, just looking for a gift for my girlfriend, she collects soft toys.'

'Right you are, 'Mr McAllister smiled and walked away.

It was now 1.10pm.

'Right Mrs Ham, is this all right for you?'

They both laughed slightly as Mrs Ham replied, 'I'd look all right on that don't you think?' Then she added, 'Josh will be thrilled, I know he will.'

'Now, this being his first real bike is the young man going to need stabilisers?'

'No, I'm not going to bother with that but I'll tell Jenny to come back to you if she decides he needs them.'

'Right you are then, it's just the balance to pay of £15.00.'

Mrs Ham produced a credit card from her purse and the amount was paid.

At 1.15 pm. Mr McAllister was waiting for the receipt and counterfoil to print when he noticed the young man heading for the shop door.

'Are you all right?' Mr McAllister asked?'

'Can't make up my mind,' the young man answered and not turning he left the shop and ran across the road to where a girl of around seventeen was waiting for him. She smiled and they went off up the street together.

Mr McAllister handed the printed receipt to Mrs Ham and wished her good day. He followed her to the door, locked it behind her and turned the sign to 'closed'. He then walked over to the soft toy section. At first everything seemed fine, and then he noticed a space. A puppy sized spaniel, a 'dangling dog', one that would hang over shelves or arms had gone. He knew who had taken it, *'The blatant, arrogant youth, while I was distracted with Mrs Ham. No wonder the girl smiled when he returned'*, Mr McAllister thought to himself, *'She'd got what she wanted to add to her collection.'*

Lunch wasn't so enjoyable that afternoon. In fact, it stuck in Mac's throat. His wife told him not to bother so much. It was after all only a toy dog. Mac replied, '*It was the principle, not what was taken that was the issue.'*

'Shall I come to the shop with you this afternoon?' his wife asked, 'You could probably do with more than just yourself, even on a Wednesday.'

His wife was quite surprised when he accepted her offer. She got herself ready and they left for the shop. They were there ready to open up at 2.15 pm.

It was a quiet afternoon and really there wasn't anything for Mrs McAllister to help with, except make cups of tea and coffee.

At a quarter past three the infants from the primary school all went by the shop with their mothers on their way home. Mr McAllister could see them from the counter and some would press their faces against the shop window and point to whatever they wanted or whatever had taken their eye. If they saw Mac they would wave to him and smile. Mac would then wave back. The children would smile again and move on.

It was at about twenty past three that Mac noticed Mrs Ham walking by with Josh, her grandson. Mac was out of sight, hidden by boxed games and model railway accessories. He gasped as he saw what young Josh had under his arm. A puppy sized spaniel, a dangling dog, *'now'* he thought, '*where's that come from? Mrs Ham was only alone while I got the bike from the stockroom, two to three minutes, no more.'*

He walked back to the counter and as he did he called to his wife, 'Joan, Joan, we'd better watch Mrs Ham in future. I've just found out she's a fast mover.'

13 JOY

Joy's son had called in to visit. It was eight-thirty in the morning. She hadn't finished breakfast when the door bell rang. She knew it wouldn't be the post, that didn't come for at least another hour, ten o'clock usually. Usually? It was always ten o'clock!

Joy had looked at her watch as she walked from the kitchen to the hall to the door. That's how she knew precisely the time of his visit. Once there she looked through the frosted glass panes in the door. It didn't make the image any clearer. It did its job, she thought, and the beginnings of a smile started. Bill, her late husband would have laughed at this. He was always amused by her idiosyncrasies and there were many along similar lines. In particular, the way she looked at an envelope and studied the writing before opening it. If she didn't recognise the writing she would say '*I wonder who it's from*?'

She was still smiling at these thoughts as she opened the door. The smile faded as she came face to face with her son, Gordon. It wasn't that she wasn't pleased to see him or that as a mother she had no time or love for him but Gordon was now forty-six, single and lived in an apartment on the other side of town, and Joy knew from experience to be wary of Gordon's early morning visits. There was usually an ulterior motive.

Gordon worked in the city. What that work

involved Joy wasn't quite sure but Gordon seemed to make a good living from it. Gordon had been married once, to Elaine. Joy had liked Elaine but after three years of marriage Gordon no longer loved her. That was twenty years ago and since then Gordon had remained 'Mr Singleton', as Joy referred to him.

Elaine and Gordon had never produced and Joy wasn't particularly broody for grandchildren. They would be nice, she thought but '*que sera sera*'.

'Gordon.'

'Mum.'

'You're not at work. Are you ill?'

'You could ask me in, please.'

'Yes, of course. Come on, tea's in the pot. I'm just finishing breakfast.'

'I'll have coffee please, black.'

'You'll make your own then. I've told you, I'm having breakfast.'

Gordon made his coffee and joined his mother at the table.

'Mum, I guess you're wondering why I've called so early but I've some news for you.'
Joy replaced her tea cup on its saucer and looked her son in the eyes.

'Yes', she said.

Gordon averted his eyes and looked at the floor. His mother knew it would be something he should have told her before but hadn't got round to. He had done this sort of thing since the age of seven when he'd had to tell his parents that he had stolen an 'Aero' bar from one of his classmates. His mother broke the silence that was becoming an awkward barrier.

'Not wanting to taste any more bubbles, Gordon?'

Gordon smiled, 'no, nothing like that.'

'What is it then?'

'There's someone I'd like you to meet.'

'Oh.'

'Her name's Sylvia. She's outside in the car.'

'Right.'

'Yes. Sylvia's waiting for me to go and get her, waiting for me to bring her to meet you.'

'Because?'

'Because?' Gordon queried.

'Yes. Why am I meeting Sylvia? You've not mentioned her before.'

'No, that's right. I've known her for about two years. We met at work.'

'Work. What is it exactly, your work?'

'We don't need to go into that now. Anyway you know I work in town at Clevedon's.'

'Clevedon's. What do they do? I've never known.'

'Medical supplies for factories and offices, all that sort of stuff.'

'Pays well does it?'

'Yes. Mum, just stop chipping in and listen. I've brought Sylvia to meet you as we're getting married at eleven-thirty. We'd like you to come.'

'Thanks for the invitation. Will you require a gift? It's such very short notice and the shops will barely be aired.'

'Mum, you'll like her. I know you will. I'll just go and get her. While I'm gone you think of something you can wear for a wedding. We'd like you to come.'

As Gordon left the kitchen his mother called after him, 'If you'd have wanted me to come to your wedding, I'd have met Sylvia and known about things before today.'

Gordon knew his mother was right. He wasn't sure he wanted her to come to the wedding. He'd rather have told her after the event. He was doing this for Sylvia. Sylvia had said she didn't want to get married without 'family' and as she hadn't any Gordon should tell his mother. She didn't think he'd leave it right until the last minute.

Sylvia was getting edgy as she sat in the car. Had the meeting gone all right? Would Joy attend their 'big day'? Sylvia was wearing a full length dress of cream lace. It buttoned down the back and fell loosely to the floor from a front yoke. The sleeves were full length with a deep cuff and fastened with tiny pearl buttons. In her hair she had pinned tiny rosebuds. On the seat beside her was her bouquet. Nothing too formal, roses of varying shades of pink and lemon. There was a buttonhole for Gordon and a corsage for Joy.

Sylvia wanted Gordon's mother to like her. To love her as she would a daughter. She looked up to see Gordon coming down the road. Was he in fair mood or foul? It was sometimes difficult to tell with Gordon. As he got nearer the car he smiled. He opened the car door and helped Sylvia out.

'Come on, mum's waiting. I've told her to put her glad rags on, she's coming to a wedding.'

Sylvia smiled. 'You told her then?'

'Yes. Come on. She wants to meet you.'

Sylvia stepped carefully up the road. She didn't want to mark her dress in any way. She felt her stomach lurch. The thought of meeting Joy was making her nervous. Gordon squeezed her hand and told her not to worry. He rang the door bell and waited for his mother to answer. She did. Joy's smile suddenly turned to a look of astonishment.

'Good Lord, Gordon. It's one thing asking me to come to your wedding, but you could have told me I was going to be a grandmother as well.'

Sylvia looked at Gordon, tears had begun to well in her eyes.

'You said you'd told her,' she said.

'Mum, keep your voice down, you've upset Sylvia. Can we come in?'

When the wedding party was assembled in the lounge, Joy felt the need to ask Gordon a few questions but she couldn't, not with Sylvia there. It would have to wait. The future Mrs Wilmore had to be considered and Joy liked to think of herself as fair in all dealings. Joy smiled at Sylvia who in turn smiled at Joy and then at Gordon. Things seem to be calmer now, Joy thought.

'Tea, coffee?' she asked.

'No, fine thanks.' Gordon and Sylvia answered together.

Joy smiled again.

'Where is the wedding? Gordon's told me the time but omitted to say where.

'It's at St Anne's, in the square. I always attend

the weekly lunchtime service and the vicar's very nice,' Sylvia responded.

'Oh, a church wedding. Good. I'll ...' Joy was interrupted by Gordon.

'I knew you'd like a church wedding. I said the same to Sylvia.'

His mother carried on.

'Before I was interrupted I was going to say, a church wedding, good. I'll wear my powder blue dress and jacket.'

'I've got you a corsage Mrs Wilmore. It's in the car, pale yellow and pink roses,' Sylvia said.

'In that case I shall wear lemon. I have a dress and jacket that screams *'wedding'* at me every time I open the wardrobe.' Joy paused and then carried on.

'Shall I wear a hat? I shall be wearing gloves, summer ones of course, but what about a hat?'

'I'd like it if you would,' Sylvia replied. 'We haven't many guests, so I'd rather like the ones we have to dress up.'

'A hat it is then. Who are the other guests? Will I know them?'

'Just friends from work,' Gordon replied. 'Sylvia hasn't any family you see. That's why everything is low key.

Joy smiled, *'how low key can you go with the bride about to give birth'*, she thought.

She said nothing. From what she'd seen of Sylvia she did seem a lovely girl and if looks were anything to go by about twenty years younger than Gordon.

'Right,' Joy said, 'I'll go and get myself ready.'

‘I like your mum,’ Sylvia said when she and Gordon were left alone in the lounge.

‘She’s ok. Can be a bit overpowering at times but I think her heart’s in the right place.’

Joy sat and looked at herself in the dressing table mirror. She ran the comb through her hair and applied her make-up. ‘I never thought I should be attending a wedding today. I wonder what Bill would have made of it all? I do wish Gordon would speak to me more, not see me as some kind of lonely old woman who only wants to speak to her son to fill in part of her day. I enjoy conversation. I could enjoy his, if he’d let me.’

Joy changed into her outfit and took her hat from the box. She had a bag and shoes that would tie in. She was sure Gordon would make some remark about the fact that she was never caught out sartorially. Joy glanced at her watch, nine thirty-seven. She’d better get a move on. She collected her things together and rejoined Gordon and Sylvia. ‘*They look content*’, she thought, ‘*they really do.*’

‘You look the part mum. I said to Sylvia that you’d have all the gear.’

Joy smiled, ‘I knew you’d comment.’

Sylvia went to freshen up, leaving Gordon and his mother together.

‘I’m surprised you’ve not said anything more,’ Gordon said.

‘What’s there to say? I wish I’d had more warning of events but surprises are good.’

‘You’ll like her. And who’d have thought I’d be a dad? I reckon I’ll be ok though.’

They heard Sylvia’s footsteps on the stairs.

Sylvia smiled as she stepped through the door to join them. Gordon took Sylvia's hand and linked arms with his mother.

'Come on then, let's get to the wedding,' he said.

Joy smiled. She was neither foolish enough nor wise enough to comment on events. She would keep mum and enjoy the day.

14 JANE SAID

Jane said our mum died of religion. She said aunty Em had died of religion too. I asked her what she meant, she said when Cousin Albert died, aunty Em kept going to the churchyard and crying, don't you remember? I didn't, and mum hadn't gone to the churchyard crying. She cried at home, when she thought we couldn't see.

Jane was twelve. I was eight, but I wasn't the baby of the family. John was. John was eighteen months old.

Jane said I had to do as I was told now mum was gone. I didn't always. Jane wasn't my mum. My mum was gone.

Mum has been gone a long time. I don't think John will ever, ever remember her. I can, but her face goes all fuzzy. I have a picture of her, dad gave me it. I look at it every night after saying my prayers. I pray for mum and dad and us and that I never catch religion. I don't want to die, I'm only eight.

Jane looks after John a lot. I don't feel sorry for her because I have to wash up after tea. Jane says I'll get into bother if I don't, when dad comes in.

He's never in! Mum used to be in all the time. She read us stories. My favourite was Cinderella. I was the princess at the end, always. She 'had a lovely frock', mum used to say. Jane would laugh and say I wasn't pretty enough to be a princess but Jane doesn't know everything. Mum used to say I was special, but that was before she got religion.

Jane makes tea for us all. She collects John from Mrs P's after school. Mrs P was a friend of gran's. Gran died after mum. She didn't have religion. I heard dad telling Mrs P once that it was a heart attack. It was a blessing he said. I wonder why? Why was it a blessing? Jane doesn't know, I've asked her, that's how I know she doesn't know everything.

It's six o'clock, we've had tea and I've washed up. I'm going to ask dad about religion. I am. I won't tell Jane. She says she's in charge until dad gets in. I don't believe her. She's just bossy.

It's nine o'clock before dad comes in. I'm in bed but I'm not asleep. Jane thinks I am. Every time she checks I just stay very still.

Sometimes I hear Jane crying. I wonder if Jane's getting religion? I know you cry when you fall but that's different. Jane never falls, so it must be religion. I'll ask dad. I never cry now, even when I fall over.

When I'm in bed I close my eyes and pretend I'm asleep. If I pretend enough maybe mum will come back. I think Jane would like that. I screw up my eyes as tightly as I can and then open them quickly. Mum's not here.

ABOUT THE AUTHOR

Margaret Holbrook lives in Cheshire.
She writes stories, plays and poetry and has had her work published in several anthologies.

In October 2012 she was a finalist in the Ovation Theatre Awards. Her short play *Soup for Starters* received an Honourable Mention.
In June 2013 her one minute play, *Talk to Me*, was a winner in the Gi60 play festival in Halifax.

Some of Margaret's work has been read on local radio.